W9-ASH-785

DREAMING OF YOU

ALSO BY MELISSA LOZADA-OLIVA

POETRY

peluda

DREAMING OF YOU

A

NOVEL

IN VERSE

MELISSA LOZADA-OLIVA

ASTRA HOUSE · NEW YORK

Copyright © 2021 by Melissa Lozada-Oliva
All rights reserved. Copying or digitizing this book for storage,
display, or distribution in any other medium is strictly prohibited.

The poetry broadside entitled "Resurrecting Selena" by Tiffany Mallery
appears courtesy of the artist.

For information about permission to reproduce selections from this
book, please contact permissions@astrahouse.com.

This book is a work of fiction. The names of some real people and places
appear in the book, but the events depicted in the book are entirely imaginary.
All the names and events in this book are the product of the
author's imagination or are used fictitiously.

Astra House
A Division of Astra Publishing House
astrahouse.com
Printed in the United States of America

Publisher's Cataloging-in-Publication Data
Names: Lozada-Oliva, Melissa, author.
Title: Dreaming of you : a novel in verse / Melissa Lozada-Oliva.
Description: New York, NY: Astra House, 2021.
Identifiers: LCCN: 2021909548 | ISBN: 9781662600593 (hardcover) |
9781662600609 (ebook)
Subjects: LCSH Hispanic American women–Fiction. | Women–Fiction. |
Grief–Fiction. | Love stories. | Lesbians–Fiction. | Novels in verse. |
BISAC FICTION / Hispanic & Latino | FICTION / Feminist | POETRY /
Subjects & Themes / Death, Grief, Loss
Classification: LCC PS3612.O9545 D74 2021 | DDC 813.6–dc23

First edition
10 9 8 7 6 5 4 3 2 1

Design by Richard Oriolo
The text is set in Century Schoolbook Std.
The titles are set in ITC Franklin Gothic.

For my sisters, Stephanie & Mariajose

CONTENTS

PART I: COMO LA FLOR, TANTO AMOR

PART II: ME MARCHO HOY

PART III: YO SE PERDER

PART IV: COMO ME DUELE

EPILOGUE

ALTERNATE ENDING

DREAMING OF YOU

CAST OF CHARACTERS

YOLANDA SALDIVAR as BFF for life and Selena's murderer, in possession of breasts and a vagina, short hair when she's a villain, long hair in a braid when she's little and playing hide-and-seek, massive manipulator, possible lesbian, behind bars, hand reaching out of the dirt with vengeance.

MAMI as smell of cloro on Sunday mornings, heavy feet thumping up the stairs, wet men's jacket hanging up to dry, sound of urine sprinkling because the door was left open, discounted bottle of wine, salty soup on a hot day, hand over the mouth because there's a pain in a tooth, bras tangled in one another and left in the dryer.

PAPI/ABRAHAM QUINTANILLA as the word "reloj," which you must learn to say if you're going to start singing in Spanish, as in, the future isn't real. The future is just a story we tell. Everything is a sign if you think about it. One day you'll be on a stage and you'll hear the applause deep in the center of you. You're the stadium. You're the emergency exit signs. You're the overpriced churros. You're the chariot led by white horses. One day you'll get news and you'll be squealing, jumping up and down, wrapping your legs around the first person you can see. You are looking up at yourself. You are about to get there. You are always gonna be my little girl.

SELENA QUINTANILLA-PÉREZ as a star I can only see because it has died. As a girl in love. As a sister and a daughter and a wife, but never a mother. As all of our dreams in the shape of a woman bleeding out on a carpet. As many old women, with wrinkled hands, dyeing white hairs. Alive and dead and in-between and always dancing.

SHE is born out of spite, the most fertile feeling. She kills her birth mother when she violently pushes the birth walls open and makes everyone scream with the branches growing out of her ears. She smells like manifested fear that is also perverse. She is the self that flares up when there is mention of somebody prettier and rattles the insides with her fists. She is what is trained out with good posture and disapproving looks. She has a photo album dedicated to humiliation that she takes out during parties. She wears a Freudian slip and loves the way her nipples feel underneath it. She is the shadow side. The bad side. Evil side. Whatever that means.

LAS CHISMOSAS as the eyes and the ears, the ones who know you before you even know you, as the stories whispered in the night and whatever lights up the asses of fireflies, as the page, indented, as the fight at the wedding and the retelling of the fight, as your tías, as your tatara abuelas, as a crumpled-up note picked up by the wrong person or perhaps the right person, the only person.

YOU as the consumer and the consumed. As the dear reader. As the drawing in the notebook and then the back of the man in the ethnic foods aisle, the stranger on the bus; in the elevator getting off before romance started, standing on top of a bucket of paint, sitting on the edge of the bed practicing your instrument, using your hands to wipe up the dust on the floor, using a blow-dryer to dry your socks, sweating deep into your shirt, faceless in an audience, face lit up by the screen.

MELISSA LOZADA-OLIVA it's been me, it's always been me. The whole time.

PART I

COMO LA FLOR, TANTO AMOR

Your music makes me feel lonely

I must be responsible for it

I'm alive

—ARIANA REINES

Hello, querido reader.
Do you like poetry?
Maybe you like songs?
Do songs get trapped in your
head like a rat on sticky paper?
Are you afraid of dying
and does it fuel you?
We aren't trying to
sell you anything,
but consider hanging us
on your wall.
Primero que todo,
we love chisme.
What is a meal
without the seasoning of gossip?
What is a conversation without
a little talking-some-shit?
We make eyes
at each other through the trees.
We clink our beers together on rooftops.
We send messages later, on the car ride home.
We all know the story of Selena Quintanilla.
The Tejana pop star who was murdered
by her best friend and the manager
of her fan club, Yolanda Saldivar.
There are heroes.
There are villains.
There are fans.
There are girls trying to find
their reflection in a rippling

pond, and then feeling startled
when a piece of gum falls out
of their mouth.
There is a frog that thinks
the gum is a fly and chokes to death.
Where were we?
This is a story of mirrors,
or what happens
when you bring the mirror
back from the dead and when
you look in it you see yourself
eating yourself.
This is about You,
except when it's not about you.
This is a love story.
But it isn't our story.
However, as chismosas, we feel
that it happened to us.
So we believe we are the best
ones to tell it.
We will try to
tell it to you
the best that we can.
First, let's introduce
our speaker, Melissa,
who does not speak
entirely for us.
She is a girl who dreams
a lot.

Dreaming of You

I want to know who the "You" is. Is it God?
Is it a Band? Is it the person we're confessing to
in a diary? My professor said second person is
useless but maybe that makes it powerful. I used to think God was
living in the glow-in-the-dark star I had stuck on the ceiling as a child
and whenever I would masturbate I'd
turn away.

Late at night when all the world is sleeping
I stay up and think that everyone I've ever loved is the same
whimsical spirit floating from one sad flesh husk to the next.
I will spoon the wall or the wall will spoon me, and all of the spirits,
every sad clown, every animated guitar, every inside joke about an arbitrary
sock will hold me until they fall asleep.

You and me are having sex to a movie.
Or during a movie?
Or at a movie?
In conversation with?
At least we're in the dark enough
so I don't have to feel bad about my body.
At least there's only this light from the actors' faces,
floating across my skin.
I'm afraid even my orgasms have dimples.

I text you, *Dang, I have plans!* but what I really mean is
what is better than me
and my imagination? What is more loving
than of all the ways I can invent You
touching me?

Regretfully, the barista who gave me
one-dollar coffees didn't have a crush on me
but was just "new" and was recently "fired"
because he "didn't know" how to "use the machine."

I saw him at the bar last night.
I waved to him. He cocked his head and turned
around.

Today,
I walked into a coffee shop
but no one was there who looked like
they could completely fuck up my life and inspire
a mediocre poem and a half so
I just left.

That was a lie.
All three of those things.

I am a poet for a living, which is not something
I ever thought could happen but alas,
I won the YouTube lottery while it
was still hot and got out before it wasn't.
I go to colleges and talk about myself

musically. I get fan mail.
I help young girls see themselves.
I guess that makes me happy.

I crave a ferry to San Francisco and a dead phone
full of messages. I'm horny for an empty chair and a street
crawling with the shadows of strangers. It feels good
to have all eyes on me. It feels better to blow
them all away like ladybugs.

I can't say for sure if I've ever had good sex.
I just know that I can enjoy myself and that afterward
there's a fertile kind of sadness.
I wish all of my friends could have sex
with my lovers so that way we could
compare notes but none of my friends are single.
I guess what I'm saying is I miss my friends.

Why are people in relationships always
taking naps?

I came to New York to get an MFA
but maybe also to fall in love?
Don't tell anyone that.
New York is cool because you only start
dating someone so that it's easier to pay the rent.
That being said my roommates are always ending things
and I can always hear them.
Anna says, "I just feel like I'm capable of feeling love
for multiple people."

Delilah's like, "But will you always love me the most?"
On and off, on and on, for days and hours. They cry and they scream
and they pull out their hair and then it gets longer.
I want to pull back the curtain that separates my
bedroom and theirs and tell them to Break Up, please.
Just kidding! It isn't a curtain.
It's a series of jackets duct taped together.
Just kidding! It's a collection of Polaroids throughout the years that
    I've strung together with twine.
Also kidding! It's just a door.
I keep it closed.

I'm watching a couple peck
each other on the cheek at a stoplight.
They're on bikes. I want to yell
"That's unsafe!" but that would
probably make it more unsafe.

If you must know, my parents
had a bad divorce when I was twelve.
But before that, they would dance
at the family functions. They would
bachata across the floor, heads together,
hands pressed against necks and backs,
sweating and swaying in this violent
way everyone always said I could sway,
because it's in my blood.
My sisters and I sat at tables lined with flowers
and plastic sheets and we would hide our faces,

embarrassed because all of the primos and tíos were watching.
And of course my parents knew that.
Then the song would end.
Then the lights would turn on and it was just them
left on the floor of the gymnasium rented out for the night,
surrounded by defeated balloons
and cake that was all crushed
strawberries and earnest whipped cream,
which is, for some reason, the way Latinos love
their cake.

This is how I like to remember it, anyway.

"Dreaming of You" was released posthumously,
which is a word that I used to believe
meant "after you were funny." If you're that
pretty can you have a good sense of humor? Come on.
I can't help but crack
the hell up listening to Selena whisper, "Como te necesito."
Is that what boys would want me to whisper into their ears? Spanish
songs are all so fucking dramatic. Everything is
a stage, I guess, or the altar we die on.

So, wring your hands at my feet!
Set some candles on my shoulders!
Place those flowers in my eyeballs, baby!
Cry over my wardrobe!
I don't know. Don't listen
to me. That won't make a good song.

How about, toward the end,

when she whispers "I love you," and answers,

"I love you too"?

It's like I can see her.

It's like she's talking to me.

It's like she's alone

in her room, in some apartment in the ceiling.

She's got her fuzzy slippers on.

She's got her hair in two tight black trencitas.

There's a green exfoliant mask settled on her moon-

face. The lights are still on because she's a girl

who is all at once confident and afraid. She's holding

up her two hands and she's pinching them into mouths.

She's making them kiss.

It's fair to say that our speaker
is in a hole
and perhaps she doesn't know
when the hole started
or when she began
her way down
but maybe
her whole life
has been a hole and the future
feels many, many holes away.
Speaking of holes—

I'm So Lonely I Grow a New Hymen

This fake little sheet strung out on the clothesline spattered with blood,
this vanilla store-bought birthday cake with my name squished on top in
    red icing,
this slime I made from an arts-and-crafts project years ago that I still keep
under my bed, this four-foot fence lined with thorny, vengeful roses,
this Dunkin' Donuts napkin Abuelita keeps in her nightstand, this sliding
    door
Mami puts a vase in front of so she can wake up if and when
there's ever a burglar, this cover ripped off from a pulp romance novel
and sent back to the publishers, these two hands joined together at
    the pinky
opening and closing to reveal a pink face faking surprise, a moist mouth
going SURPRISE! Hello what is up how is it going?
It really has been so long and I just want to tell you something.
Sometimes I miss the heartbreak of starting over.
Sometimes I really believe I can turn anything into a you.
Sometimes I want to be what breaks open and stains the sheets.

My Sisters and I Would Watch
the Selena Movie

I can pull the film over my legs
I can model it around the living room
for feedback, wait for
the "Yes, girl!"
the, "That's it!"

I'm sad we will never
be together in a room
just the same way.

All of us followed
a photo of our hearts
dragged by a string
into the dark.
All of us had our arms out,
hands reaching.

What to do when it's just
us and the photograph?

When we call out to
our sisters and they are
not there?

It's easy to make your own
light.

It's harder to face yourself
alone in the dark.

The movie ends and the
tape spits itself out.

"Again?"
Again.

We lean on one
another.
The screen moves
across our faces.
If you took
a photo from
afar, we all
look like the
same daughter.

Maybe there are holes in
all of us, just like
the Real Slim Shady.
It's only a matter
of how you fill those holes
before somebody puts a hole in you
and all of a sudden you're bleeding
out on the carpet of a hotel room,
amiright ladies? Ha.
What we mean to say is that
she tried going on a few dates.

6'5" Looking for Something Casual that Has the Potential to Be Something More ;)

[In a dimly lit restaurant]

Is this a date?

[Walking back to a car in a dark parking lot with a gun to my back]

Is this a date?

[In the trunk of a car]

Is this a date?

[In a room, tied to a chair with one, dangling light bulb]

I actually would say that I'm like, an introverted extrovert.

[Locked in an attic dressed up as a doll with a bowl of water and a plate of food at my feet]

Yeah, I don't know, I just have such a weird relationship with social media!

[In a submarine unaware of what day it is]

I'm trying this cleanse, have you heard of it?

[Chopped up into little pieces and dispersed into the ocean, little fishes feeding on my hands]

So, do you have any siblings?

She is so lucky to be born here.
She is so child-of-the-internet
she is so enlightened and not
calling her mother back
that she feels she can reclaim every word.
Loneliness
is such a right, she thinks.
The choices, the conquering, the endless night.
The trying to sleep next to a
stranger wondering if she
could have just
done this by herself,
but then if nobody
is kissing her
how can anybody prove
she's really there?

I Watch Selena's Open-Casket Funeral

I ask Mami why it was like that. Open casket. She tells
me that's just the way we do it—*we look death in the face.*
She doesn't know about the death industry. The money

made from pumping a body full of pink liquid, how they
peel a face off then back on, prick needles into the corners
of eyes to make you look like you're sleeping.

At night she will pace her empty house with the lights on,
holding her hand to her chest, while her heart thumps wildly,
trying to believe in the glass of water in her hand. Mariajose asks me
    if I ever
get those scary feelings that jerk me awake before I fall asleep.

While driving, Stephanie tells me not to put my feet up
on the dashboard because if there's a car accident—*God forbid*—
my legs will break backward. Abuelita needs a note from the doctor

in order to get her citizenship. The note reads *seemed very nervous,*
was looking around and scratching her scalp, picking her nails,
    perhaps signs
of early dementia. Olivia says if I ever find her body hacked to bits

in a ditch, most likely it was a man who did it. On Super Bowl Sunday
Stephanie sends us a picture of her husband with his tongue
out, all goofy, all playful, gripping a bloody package of ribs.

The word *carne* means meat, but also flesh. Mami taught me
this when she described the way a sewing needle pierced the space
between her thumb and pointer finger. It's very easy to picture myself
    inside

every white van I walk by; tied up in the back, twitching and screaming.
Or at the bottom of every lake. Or just choking
on a piece of lonely pasta. I can see myself bleeding out on a motel's clean
    carpet.

I can see myself crying over a body but also being the body.
I can see the way I must look to my mother, my Abuelita,
my sisters, my friends, my fans. Here is my corpse, modest

in royal purple. Here's my flower, resting against my chest.
Here are my lips, locked and painted red. Here are my rogue
baby hairs, gelled in a perfect curl. Here are my almond eyes, closed.

I am so safe.

Zombies are so totally out
and basically a fear-mongering
tool to get you to filter your
water or not vaccinate
your kids. We are not
saying we don't trust
the government. Not this time.
This time we are
saying . . . don't you ever feel like
people would care about
you more if you were dead?

Just to Make Things Clear,
I Am Not a Haunted Person

It's always my mom or my sisters who see women in gowns, standing over their beds saying their name, who, when a glass breaks or a pair of pants rips, say, "I had a dream about this," who tell me of seeing Abuelita dance with skeletons and gravestones through our door and out the window, who know that the dogs need to take a shit just by the way their eyes look, who feel

that there are cats sleeping underneath the porch just because of the way wind dances outside, who kiss people and just "get a certain feeling," who have a dream about their tights ripping and then the next day there's the tear, who believe that the dead aren't really dead but whistling at them from the trees, who move through their lives following the trail of salt in front of them, trusting it will take them somewhere with sun.

I've never felt leaves winking at me.
I do not carry crystals in my pockets.
I buy candles and forget to light them.
I've let an iced coffee mold over my tarot deck.
I record everything compulsively.
I want to leave everything behind.

What If Selena Taught Me How to Fake an Orgasm

If you are on top, she would say, make the sound
an umbrella does when it's being opened up inside.
If he's taking you from behind, turn into
a branch with eyeballs for leaves. Blink.
If his head is in between your legs, she would tell me,
give birth to the scene in *Armageddon*
where Ben Affleck uses Liv Tyler's body
as a valley for his animal crackers.
If you are in public, invite everyone you know.
Bring masks you can slip on and off.
Wear your tap dancing shoes.
Wear a tall hat.
Put something groovy on that won't make you
want to cover your ears, jump up and down, and scream
later, when you hear it in the feminine products aisle at the CVS.
Turn on the smoke machine.
Now, the stage lights pour through every orifice of your body.
Now, you are dripping with mirrors.
Now, there are flowers at your feet and rabbits scurrying
around you making more rabbits.
The moment is here, she'd let me know.
And by this time she is proud of me.
I will have trained for this.
Everyone is in my head, including me.
Listen to all that applause, crawling out of my own mouth.

Melissa moves to a new apartment.
She is looking for a change.
She is looking for a new start.
She is invited to a party
next door. Whoop-whoop. Friday night.
Too much pressure. She leaves and then
she comes back. She gets too drunk.
There is a boy with a party hat.
He is talking to her about
eggs. She asks him if it's his
birthday; he's like, no.

El Chico del Apartamento 512

What is a power couple
and how many watts do they have?
and do they need to plug themselves in?
and is it 2- or a 3-prong that they need 'cause
I dunno what I have on me, you know, ha-ha.

Anyway, I am married to all of the outlets
underneath the table.
Anyway, I want to make out
with all of my unread e-mails.
Anyway, how often have you
given someone your password to everything?

I wanna jump rope with every cable—sometimes I'm wild.
I haven't updated my phone in 52 weeks—I'm waiting for something,
I don't know what.

Do you ever feel that way sometimes?
Do you think that's quirky?
Would you want to know me?

Anyway, it's nice to meet You.
How do You know
Paula and Greg?

Karaoke Interlude

Tonight it's somebody's birthday
or it's nobody's birthday or it's the anniversary
of the third or fourth time we heard this song.
Some of us sit all night flipping through the binder
either because we don't want to embarrass
ourselves tonight or because we are trying
to find The Song, one that we can sing well
but one that everyone
will join in on, too.

Someone sings a song we don't know and we turn away
and talk shit but still feel happy for them.
For a moment we can become someone else.
What's the difference between anyone
and an Elvis impersonator?
Us and acned tweens dancing in front of the TV,
Us and bloated men with toothpicks on the long truck ride home,
Us and manic single moms slicing carrots by the sink,
Us and horny middle schoolers sweating to "Stacy's Mom."

Maria's singing "Gasolina" by Daddy Yankee
because it's the only song they have in Spanish,
and also, weirdly, she likes it.
Hannah's singing The Calling because finally, they're in love.

Don got here early and has been practicing "Strange" by Patsy Cline
   all week.
Monica, who leads Drag Trivia, is drunk again and yelling at everybody.
Puloma knows all the words to "Careless Whisper" and doesn't need to
   look at the screen.
No one likes Courtney but when she sings "Tears Dry on Their Own"
her hair flies behind her, her pink Doc Martens shine.
When Linda goes up everybody goes quiet
because she can actually sing.

For now, we are Jenny, Patsy, Daddy, Florence, Carly, Robyn, Mariah.
I do not sing Selena because she's too on the nose.
It will always be now
and we can't do anything about it.
It is now until it is another now,
shaking its head at now,
making deals with now,
turning past now because
it doesn't recognize Now, anymore.
And we are always trying to find the right song.
What is the word for getting
someone to fall in love with us during karaoke?
We know that if somebody loves us,
if they really really love us,
they're watching us and every bad thing that ever happened to us sing.

Everything is a regurgitation of something that once lived better.
We practice into our phones all week
and play back our own tiny little voices.

We channel the past through us and throw it at the Present,
which boogies, whether we want it to or not, into the future.
All of us are standing on the Present's stage
as it hurtles upward,

how we stop feeling the jolt after a while, the rise,
how it slows down the more we sing,
how we keep looking down
as the words scroll up
because they won't let us forget them.

Melissa thinks wanting
to be loved
is just wanting
to be watched
all the time.
She moves as if
she is always
on his
TV screen.
When he looks at her,
the beginning
of a song starts
to play. Somewhere,
a finger pushes a
tape in and a screen
starts to buzz.
This is a feeling
somebody has felt
before but she still
thinks it belongs to her.
She listens to the last
concert again, dances
to it alone in her room.

Crush Sonnets

I.

ME: Oh, hi! Uh. What are you doing here?

YOU: I'm food shopping. For food. Uh, to eat it.

ME: Wow, wild. Um. I do that all the time!

YOU: Do you have a favorite food . . . to eat?

ME: Yeah. I could think of a few. Not picky.

YOU: Me too. Well, I don't eat meat.

ME: Yeah, same! Or, I make vegan choices.

YOU: Would you ever want to eat something?

ME: I mean, I eat. All the time. Do you mean—

YOU: Together. If you're interested, that is.

ME: I'm interested. Definitely.

YOU: Cool. Well, see you around. Oh, sorry.

ME: Oops, I thought you were going to the left—

YOU: No, that was my bad. Please, after you.

II.

ME: We haven't touched each other all day.

YOU: Wanted to make sure it was mutual.

ME: So, we'll sleep stiff. Like we're made of metal.

YOU: Yeah, just two robots who are not touching.

ME: We could hold each other's pinkies. Like this.

YOU: I like that. But now the seal is broken.

ME: Oh no! Disastrous consequences.

YOU: I'll never see a unicorn again.

ME: Do you ever feel like you don't belong?

YOU: Like you're an alien or something?

ME: Like any second someone could notice.

YOU: You smell good. Can I come closer to you?

ME: What if I told you I was abducted?

YOU: Then aliens did a good job with you.

III.

ME: Let's play a game. Who are those people?

YOU: An old couple on their way to the movies.

ME: What are their names? What do they fight about?

YOU: Lorraine and Georgia. They . . . fight about time.

ME: Who do they miss and why don't they see them?

YOU: Their son Edgar. He went off to the big city.

ME: But I thought we were in the big city!

YOU: There's another big city, up in space.

ME: Ohhhh, back to aliens, I see. What's Edgar like?

YOU: Edgar is a dancer and he never dreams.

ME: So when he closes his eyes what happens?

YOU: Just wet darkness. Just the shadow of stars.

ME: If I were a stranger who would I be?

YOU: A funny woman I'd like to talk to.

I'm Not a Virgin But

I want to appear to You in sandwiches,
water markings on the ceiling,
mold above the toilet,
patterns in woven baskets,
a scatterplot depicting
the correlation between people who lick
their ice cream and people who bite
their ice cream and whether or not they lie
about how many books they've read.

I want you to gather strangers around
the image of me because you've gotta
make sure it's me and not a trick
your eyes are playing on You.

And I want the strangers to confirm your vision,
I want them to tell tales about me,
I want endless products in the shape of me
available in delis and on the side of the road,
I want to be the one abuelitas light candles beneath
and I want to be the picture on the candle, stretched out
and replicated, I want to be the one who gets daughters
into colleges with full rides,
brings the GoFundMe page to completion,
gets shoved
into the backpack during the big flood,
gets hanged

from doorknobs in new apartments
as a sign of protection, as a sign that
whoever lives there is loved.

I want everyone to believe in me eventually
but I want it to be You
who finds me, plain as day,
blooming among the flowers,
shining from the hill,
taking shape everywhere I shouldn't,
obvious and made of light.

Of course he loves her back.
They are pájaritos.
Little lovebirds
vibrating next to
one another in their
cages as the day
turns into the night.
Time passes.
Y el tiempo?
Se pasa y se pasa.
Because of that
she is lucky,
but a part of her
still remains
in the hole.
There are worms
here, now.

The Future Is Lodged Inside of the Female

the female is me, ripping off this skin and trying to make the perfect empanada.

passive tense because who did the lodging?
or was it self-inflicted lodging? victim
is suffering. victim pronounced dead on arrival.
lodge big. lodge for the forgotten ones. lodge like it's 1995.

would be nice to advance and upgrade but i'm just not feeling it today!
also then i can't claim to be marginalized so, uh, whatever.

in the future, i am not Spanish or Latina or Latinx instead i am:
HIS(PANIC)ED
-ED because past tense because colonialism. as in, my identity is
    something that *happened* to me.
-PANIC to acknowledge crippling anxiety, lol

here is a haiku:

somewhere in the world
there is a cishet white man
apologizing

that *is* a haiku and i *will* get the attention i deserve.

i want to turn the meat sack i live in into something more efficient
something that pops up toasted bread and tells you what's trending today

how many ways can i pull off my brand?

i have tweezers, sharp keys, an x-acto knife.

i'm okay with living

with the gaping wound and then the scar tissue and the story to have
    prepared

when people point and say

what happened there?

my work is all puns stapled together into the shape of a woman

who is really listening to you and laughing at all the right times

i'm sorry this isn't about my mom's accent enough

or the way my father dilutes it

i'm sorry this isn't about the ten occurrences of microaggressions i can
    think of off the top of my head

(are you with him or the cleaning service?)

(i'm just as dark as you in the summertime so people think I am
    Colombian)

(you're smarter than the other Latinos in this class)

okay so maybe like, three?

another haiku:

somewhere in the world

Lena Dunham is naked

apologizing.

my bad, you asked me to make this more *political and aggressive.*

so, i'm turning the phrase *it's up to you i'm down for whatever* into a
machete

and hacking at an ATM until i can pay the train fare it took me to get
here. thanks!

realizing that all my life i've been trying to look like Selena?
is Selena the hole that's been carved out for me? i can jam
my body through it but i'll probably fall to the other side.
is my body Selena-adjacent?

the female is 23, hispanic(ed), with a bullet wound to the back.
the female is 45, hispanic(ed), crying in her car with a gun.
the female cannot have a lover if she is busy finding herself.
the female cannot have a lover if she is busy finding herself!
the female killed her best friend, because only one woman can exist at a
time, whoops!
honestly so sad that she's dead but like, what if she lived long enough to
like a tweet from a pro-life organization idk?

i am deep inside now, with my fists, no gloves on!
i am doing everybody a favor!
the future is right past my reach and the size of a walnut!
the future is an illusion and i am
stuck picking our fingernails in the present.
the future is telling me to hold my identity still
so i am going to dig back into the past where it just started shaking.
the future snores in my neck and loves me back!
no, that is too much to ask of the future!

yes, the future thinks about other people! you can't stop that!
the future is in my hands now and won't stop making noise!
can someone help me turn it off? please.

my last haiku, i promise:

somewhere in a room
i am making a bad choice
for no good reason

You should never
bring
somebody back
from the dead.
Hasn't everybody seen
the remake
of Pet Sematary?
Jesu Christo.

Resurrecting Selena

MY REASONING

Because it is not enough to be seen.

Because I need to see.

Because I miss her even though I've never met her.

Because it had to be me
because if it wasn't
then it would've been
somebody else.

THE MEDIUM

I'm tired of feedback and I'm addicted to the internet. If someone else gets involved it would just be too messy. I need flowers, I need a moonlight dance, I need a song to sway to and access to wifi. I do some research. I go down YouTube holes. I come up with my own method.

HOW I BROUGHT SELENA BACK

1. Grow out my hair, purchase chunky gold hoops, buy some bright red lipstick that will stain. This is mainly for effect but it can't hurt.

2. I sing backward into a recording device and then play the recording device backward.

3. I can't tell my friends anything about this because they would think I'm nuts.

4. So I get rid of my friends.

5. I take out a loan and turn my bedroom into a lab. I take a USB drive full of Selena's images, songs, and interviews and put it into a pot of my period blood. After three weeks, roots begin to grow at its ends. I set up a table. I draw a figure on the table using lipstick.

6. I sing backward into a recording device and then play the recording device backward.

7. There's more to do. I wake You up and ask You to quickly think of the name of the girl in elementary school with the prettiest handwriting.

8. I walk into the kitchen, tie a red string around my finger, say this girl's name five times while spraying Fabuloso into the air. You walk in on me and are all, "What are you doing?"

9. I spray You in the face because I am a reactive person.

10. I run away because I am a reactive person.

11. I come back because I've thought about what I've done.

12. Days go by. Finally, it is midnight and storming. I take the USB out of the pot of period blood and I put it in some soil. I add fertilizer. I've never been good at waiting.

13. There is a cracking in the air. The walls are vibrating and I am holding the whole room together. I am on the ceiling and underneath the basement floor. There's a rapid knocking on the sliding screen door. A scream coming from the pot. My cat hisses. The lights turn on and off. I am in the closet spying and outside of the closet feeling like I'm being watched. Now it is midnight. I open a

girl-shaped door. The knob holds my hand. A cloud of pink is in front of me, rising from the table. The kind of stuff that leaks from attics. I put my hand in and scream.

13a. Now I am in a white dress running among the trees. You are behind me holding up a jukebox and it's playing something with drums.

13b. You lose me among the trees. I hear You calling my name. I want You to keep chasing me and I don't want you to know how far I would go to find out the truth of something, to scratch an itch that will tear the whole universe open. I'm sorry about this but I'm not sorry about this. I'm already lighting the candles. I'm drawing a circle in the dirt with salt. I'm taking off my shoes. I'm already feeling the dirt beneath my feet dance.

I'm Not Sure What to Do with Her, Exactly

She is sitting in my living room, legs
crossed, then legs uncrossed. I'm pacing.
You are calling and I'm ignoring. She doesn't smell
weird. There isn't any dirt on her pantsuit
or any worms crawling out of her ears.
The only spooky or weird thing
is that she looks kind
of busy. Does it make sense
when I say busy? Like, a video
I took on my phone and then uploaded to my computer
but it wasn't during prime daylight so there's this fuzzy
quality to it, like there's a billion tiny little bugs
making up the colors
on my screen. I ask her if she wants
some water.
I start to cry.
I can't believe she's touching my stuff.
Everything I've refused to throw away
because I'm too sentimental
Selena and my Trash.
Selena and my discounted tampons.
Selena and my poems.
I write poems, I tell her. *It's nothing.*
I want to show her everything.
I'm trying to be a good host. I say this out loud. She laughs
big and loud like saying that just now was the most astute,
the most real,

the most human thing,
like she never thought about it
like that before. I ask her what
she missed the most
about like, being alive.
She stops and looks
down at her fingers. They remind me of my sister's—
thin and long.
A billion tiny little bugs.
She opens her mouth.

El Chisme According to Others:
Selena at the Halloween Party

Monica, 22

All I remember thinking is "Who is this bitch?" She was
flirting with my boyfriend . . . we were already in a fight,
whatever, I was in a bad mood to begin with, and she kept
laughing at everything he was saying, just laughing, laughing.
Also she had the audacity to keep asking to change the
music . . . something about a washing machine? . . . kept asking
about "where the dancing was." Like, there doesn't have to be
dancing at a party. Sometimes it makes people uncomfortable.
I don't know, am I being defensive right now? When she
laughed I heard it in my hands.

Alexis, 28

So here is where it gets spooky, okay? I was dressed like Selena
because that's what I do every year. I had the high black pants.
The bustier and the red lipstick and even that hat. My friend
brought me to this party and we were only gonna be there for
an hour because it was just a bunch of white people hanging
around playing Catan and I was trying to get my booty rubbed.
I was adjusting my lipstick and checking to see if there was any
on my teeth and then there was this pounding on the door.
That's what I remember, this pounding. Like bam-bam. I was
like "gimme a second" and the pounding kept going so I opened
the door all annoyed and then I'm face to face with her. She
looked at me like she knew me. Her head kept moving around

as if it were bopping to a beat but every time it moved it was like those Animorph book covers, do you know what I'm talking about? Like when the girl is running but she turns into a cat if you keep moving the book around. I loved those books when I was a kid. Can't really remember what they were about.

Dan, 29

I was a Dead Poet Society? Yeah, it was really last minute. I got lazy. I wore a turtleneck and drew bags under my eyes? And my glasses. I carried around my copy of *The Odyssey*. Uh . . . yeah, so what happened? I was really surprised that she came up to me 'cause she was like, pretty hot. Everything I said she thought was like, really funny. I don't know where my girlfriend was. Sometimes it's nice when a girl just laughs. I feel kind of bad about this next part. Okay so . . . she kinda motioned toward me like "Let's go over here." Next thing I know we are in this closet and some towels fell on my head. That's when I was like, "Hey, don't I know you from somewhere?" She kissed me without asking. She asked if I could use my hands. I grabbed her bra thing—it was like those spiky sand things at the science museum. She asked me if I could "feel it too." I did not know what she meant. Most of the time it was like I was kissing a fuzzy version of a girl. But then I looked down and my hand was holding all of these worms. Freaky. Then she was just gone.

PART II

ME MARCHO HOY

Selena and Me

At first, she cannot talk. Everything she says sounds
recorded, like I've heard it before. And I have.

Me siento muy excited. Donde esta el script?
She can only say what she's said before.

Interviews, songs. *Pizza*, she keeps saying, *pizza*.
So I order us a pie. She wolfs it down.

Her skin flashes cheese and pepperoni. I turn on that Netflix
special that gives a rundown of the last thirty years of history.

There's a horrifying dial-up sound coming from her mouth
when she learns that Princess Diana died. Then Michael Jackson.

I put a finger to my mouth and shake my head.
I know, I tell her. I know.

I don't want her to wake up my roommates.
You call me again. I ignore.

I start to fall asleep. I am exhausted.
I leave my laptop open for her.

I do not think Selena sleeps, and anyway, when I'm around
her it's like the TV is always on, even when it's not.

You always said leaving the TV on is
a good way to invite spirits into the room.

All of those wavelengths, You told me.
You call me again. I turn my phone over.

Selena on the Train

Daylight. I give her a pair of jeans and a jacket
to cover up the busyness of her.
Now she looks like me.
Now we are just two girls walking down the street.
We go to the subway.
She doesn't pay the fare.
She just walks through the turnstiles.
We wait for the train.
She doesn't ask me where we're going.
She still doesn't really know what's going on.
She opens her mouth and the *Breaking Bad*
theme song comes out. I look around, freaked.
How much Netflix did she watch?
I feel a pang of guilt, like when I realized
it was too late to start letting my cat outside
because he just doesn't know enough at this
stage in his life. He would just die.
I am motherly in this way.
I am responsible.
I take out my headphones.
I put one in her right ear. She listens.
Her hair seems to glow.
She follows me onto the subway.
I wonder if anybody else can feel the buzzing.
The flickering that's beginning at her cheekbones.

I want to touch her hand but what would happen?

Would it feel like ice?

Would I be electrocuted?

Would it go right through hers?

Hi, Uh, Hi, Hello, You've Reached Melissa

You have left me many voice mails.

You just wanted to know what was going on.

I can't believe You still leave voice mails. What is that?

I feel a rush of affection for You, because You leave voice mails.

Sometimes in the voice mails You describe what you are looking at.

You are narrating a scene for me.

There is a couple dancing below the train tracks, You tell me.

They want to be ironic but they are so in love they are not.

There is a little boy holding a pigeon in Washington Square Park.

Now the little boy is setting the pigeon free.

Now is he walking away with his mother.

He is looking back at the pigeon.

The pigeon is unidentifiable among a family, a league of city pigeons.

Call me, please, You say.

Selena and You

Selena is sitting on my bed,
one hand holding *A House of My Own* by Sandra Cisneros

and the other petting my cat,
whose fur stands up with static with each rub.

I show her my favorite part.
The part about how the witch's broom

is the heart that takes us where we need to go.
Her skin looks less electric now.

Softer. Like a mask.
It scares me a little to look at her.

I tell her she can keep my jeans.
I got them fitted for me.

Jeans have never fit like that ever and I mean ever
but they look better on her.

Like they belonged to her always.
I give her a band t-shirt.

I tell her I want her to meet somebody special.
When You open Your door You look like

You're going to faint and then that stops.

You are somebody who does not ever seem surprised.

Selena embraces You, gives You a kiss on the cheek.

"*I'm really tired,*" she says, "*Los labios. Hola.*"

I look at You and You look at me.

I am excited. Two worlds meeting.

You go to the sink and pour a large glass of water.

You do not say anything to me.

I Take Selena to a Poetry Reading

Tonight I'm performing at The Bell House, which is a huge deal for me.
When Selena gains more language she asks the inevitable question.
"What do you do?"

Any time somebody asks me this I can only shit out an answer,
leave it there, and walk away, ashamed.
I tell her I am a poet.

She says, "That's romantic!"
I tell her that I go to colleges and universities and I read poetry there
and that's how I make a living.

She doesn't care. She didn't ask about that.
"So you do what you love!"
She gives me a hug.

She is starting to have a scent now.
I breathe it in her hair.
"Your Mami must be so proud of you."

She squeezes my arm.
And even if she isn't, it feels true.
Even if I don't feel in love, I believe in it.

I think of her when I take the stage.
I think of her when the audience feeds me their laughter
and the mmms from their empathetic throats.

I invited You but I could not reserve
You a seat. Selena's coming, I tell You.
You watch from the back.

In the Middle of My Poem

Selena jumps on stage.
She is like a child. Head in her hands,
feet moving back and forth behind her.
The audience starts to murmur.

Somebody says, "Is that who I think it is?"
Selena stands up.
She rips the microphone from me.
"Melissa is my inspiration!"

She tells the audience,
"Believe in yourself!
Follow your dreams!
Do what you LOVE!"

Love echoes throughout
the venue. It touches every
audience member on the cheek.
They all stand up.
I watch them.
The lights blink on and off.

They begin to scream.
"SELENA!" I hear.
My Latina fans with their
septum piercings and purple in their hair
sob loudly.

Selena laughs. A big, real laugh
that I feel in my groin.
She is laughing and the lights are blinking.
She flicks her hair back and it hits me in the face,
black tentacles slashing
me and making themselves known.

A Star Is Born Again

INT. NIGHT TIME. MELISSA'S APARTMENT.

MELISSA *and* SELENA *watch the video someone put on the internet of* SELENA *saying* "LOVE" *on* MELISSA'S *laptop.* MELISSA'S *phone rings.*

REP'S VOICE
Saw that video. Really excited
about what I saw there. I'm calling
with great interest in representing
Selena.

MELISSA *passes* SELENA *the phone.*

SELENA
Hello? This is me?

SELENA *leaves* MELISSA'S *apartment.* MELISSA *watches* SELENA *pace outside through the window. She twirls her long, black hair in her fingers.* SELENA *returns, jumps on* MELISSA'S *bed, squealing.*

SELENA
They want me to go on tour!

MELISSA *tries to hide her jealousy.*

MELISSA

A tour? Wow. Amazing. Could I come?

SELENA *puts her hands on* MELISSA's *shoulders.*

SELENA

Of course you can come.
You are my best friend.

MELISSA's *phone rings again. An unknown number.*

ABRAHAM QUINTANILLA

Put my daughter on the phone NOW!

MELISSA *knows who it is. She hands the phone back
to* SELENA. *It's her whole family. They are crying
loudly on the other end.* MELISSA *is losing* SELENA
before SELENA *knows to be gone. She brushes her
hands through her hair. Strands, thick as
spaghetti, come out in her hands.*

It started to happen
after all of that
but maybe it had been
here the whole time.
She thought it skipped her—hearing sadness
in the wind, but then
she realizes that she is
the wind, or the lady
with the large cheeks
at the end of the world
blowing until she passes out.
She is overwhelmed.
She leaves to go for a walk
around her neighborhood,
clear her head.
It's very dramatic.
When she comes back Selena is gone

Selena Asks for Directions

A normal day for me is (sleep sounds)
Like Oh my god que esta pasando.
Que vamos hacer, donde esta el script?
No, don't worry about it. Aplausos.
Soy muy sorprendida. Hey, you got it.
I'm really tired. Los labios. Hola.
It was great it's an honor. No se.
I have the key to the city here.
It's SELENA. You've known me forever.
Lipstick down here from microphone, ha-ha.
So I just want to let you know that
I forgot to bring up my hands. I know that
everybody's gonna watch this
So I'm smiling for everybody

I Try to Go On with My Life

I had a panic attack on the F train.
I crouched with my head in my hands while
wheezing and said "Oh my God" fifteen times.
No one did anything but it made me
feel stronger.
I started going to the gym because
I want a tight ass and a tight mind but I am
very loose morally and also like, physically?
My biggest fear is getting raped and murdered
and then getting ripped
to shreds on the internet.
I think of small talk and romance as the same thing.
I mean to say: I am charming, I don't know what to do
with this napkin, now please go away.
I'm doing my taxes and I'm nostalgic for all the times
I spent money with You.
I don't know how to say this without saying this.
Every bar in Brooklyn smells like the same
type of fries. I have a sense
of humor but it's
probably a crutch for something deeper.
New York is an inside joke you have to pay for.

When we go to sleep, what happens?
Vengeful clowns. uneatable cake.
Running as if you are underwater.
Kissing people you didn't know
you wanted to kiss.
Melissa's dreams shift.
Late at night
while all the world
is sleeping, we wait
outside. Our nails are
long and our eyes are sharp.
We are listening.
We are looking.
Melissa has a visitor

I Will Name It She

One night She is there, hovering above me.
I will say that She
is in the shape of me.

At night, She floats over me and
I see the hairs growing on her chin,
smell the stench from her mouth.
She really makes me hate me.
What I notice the most is the noise radiating from her pussy.
It somehow sounds like:

- Somebody Leaving Me in the Middle of the Night
- Everybody I Care About Dying
- My Writing Up in Flames
- The Phrase "Can I Give You Some Feedback?"

She will stand on the bed while You
snore next to me, one arm over your eyes,
like You're dreaming
about being on the beach where the sun
is so hot, so bright in this lucky way
that you just can't stand.
You just cannot stand all of your good
luck. Oh, I am so jealous of You sometimes.

We all have holes
and we are all a little
Haunted. When was a time you
felt afraid for no reason and why?
Some people say scary stories
make them feel horny.
It's that adrenaline.
The knowledge
that the man in
the corner of the room
was really a lamp.
The doll winking at
you was just a trick of the light.
The strangers holding
knives at your throat
were part of a bad dream.
You were just dreaming, nena.

Who's That Girl?

Sitting at a coffee shop, a man taps me from behind. When I turn around he says, *I'm sorry, you look just like the person I was meeting, but from behind.* I'm like, *Don't worry about it.* The person who walks in through the coffee shop doors and makes the bells jingle is Your ex-girlfriend, who sent You an e-mail last fall saying she hoped You'd *disappear* inside of my *inspiring vagina.* I'm thinking, the drama. I'm thinking, the big coincidence of my life. The story I will tell later, to my friends. Of course she has a name but for now she is The Girl Who Looks Just Like Me But from Behind. I'm sitting next to them, the man and The Girl Who Looks Just Like Me But from Behind, for two hours. I find that I can't turn to look at her face, which is fine because any acknowledgment from either of us would reveal all of the hours on the internet, a window of the rabbit hole the other went down. I am frozen in front of my things. I am listening to her go on about her life. Which is a little like my life except it's her life. She is doing really well. She is starting a jewelry business. Okay. Later that day, while waiting for the train, a woman waves at me at the end of the platform. She pushes past all the commuters. She is all flushed when she arrives, all excited, all out of breath. Then she shakes her head. *I'm sorry*, she says. *Your hair, your glasses.*

Days go by. I eat dinner. I brush my teeth. I lotion my ankles. One afternoon, in the middle of telling me about a BDSM party they went to, my friend asks me, *Wait, did I tell you this already? Or was that somebody else?* A car drives by me while I'm on my bicycle. A bunch of phones stick out the window. I hear clicking. In bed You tell me I smell different. I'm like *Bad different?* You're like, *Not good or bad. Just different.* More days, more nights. My hair falls out at a usual rate. The dog I usually pet on my way to the deli starts barking at me. Inside of the library elevators, nobody knows who wants to get to the eleventh floor. My students continue their conversations when I arrive. I cook food and it keeps missing my mouth. My cat looks out the window like I'm about to come home even though I'm right there. Onstage, I take a deep breath. Begin my poem. Try to not just recite it. Feel it this time. Remember the person I was when I wrote it. I hear sipping from a beer can. The crossing and uncrossing of legs. I finish. Nobody claps. Nobody cheers. Someone whispers to the person who dragged them here, *When is the show supposed to start?* One morning I look up at the mirror from washing my face and it's like my face is scrolling upward, like someone else's thumb is pushing it there. I try to hold it down.

Mami Calls Me to Tell Me
She Had a Dream

You were little again and wearing a yellow jacket.
We are in a department store.
You were there and you were not.
I keep looking for the yellow jacket.
I ask the shoppers.
Have you seen my little girl?
Have you seen her?
Where did she go?
I lost you and I didn't
have a picture of you
to show them.

If You Could Give It a Name,
Who Would She Be?

I write it down on my hands in Sharpie. Someone uses it
                              as an excuse to touch me.
              What does this mean?

              I pin it down and place it in a petri dish.
        I hang
it on my wall,   in a collection of everything else
                        I have a word for

              (a picture of somebody else crossed out with red).

I leave the room,
                        I close
the door,
              I leave my house
my wallet in one pocket
my phone in the other,
                                   I make my way
                        to the train.
                        Something starts
to twitch.
                        Something starts
to tap at the glass.

              I am holding a bag of myself over a high building!
              I am shaking the bag!

I am in pieces, falling all over the sidewalk!
I am so thin, finally!
I am landing on cars!
I am getting stuck in bushes!
I am making people squeal!
I am waiting for You to grab at me!
to gather what You can!
to stuff me in Your pockets!
to take me home and put me!
under your mattress! hurry up!
please hurry up please!
where are you please!
there is only!
so much of me left!

Catching my breath and tying it to a tree.

It's happening, phones off, it's happening, legs crossed, it's
    about to happen.

Papi once rolled down the window.
He breathed faster and held on to his chest.
Hands in Papi's chest, clapping.
Papi pulled over to a Walgreens.
There was an ambulance.
I walked into the Walgreens.
Papi was holding his chest on the floor.
It's okay. It's okay. It's okay.

I don't know   I don't know   I don't know   but can
    You please not leave me alone?

        Meli, what is happening in that big brain of yours?

Everything bad about me,
                escaping out of the dishwasher
                                with spindly legs.

If you must know YEAH it is like this   all the time.

Trying to protect myself, I let out really bad things.

        Your dad is gonna be fine. Someone else should
        drive him home, though.

                        asking my breath to the prom
                        using empty cans and string
teaching my breath how to ride a bicycle.
                    singing with my breath in the shower
lying under my breath.
                            checking my breath.
losing my breath.
                        telling my breath the plot to *Jaws*.
crossing the street with my breath.
                sharing my breath with someone else in a
                room with cold air.
feeling it rise.

I hold it in my hand.

It's wet and pulpy.

It writhes and hisses and I am not
          strong enough to squeeze.

I want to help you,

but I can't help you if you can't

tell me how

to

Papi Calls Me

but I cannot answer the phone. I want to,
but I can't. He calls again. He texts me.
He wants to know why I'm ignoring him.
He says,
I am watching CNN and today is
about NYU medical students.
All medical students have tuition for
free. Would you consider being a doctor?
Lol I hope.

Things aren't going so well
with the You. ¡Que pena!
Mostly because
he can't see her anymore and when
he does all they do is fight.
He is concerned with what happened
that night with the candles.
But the You has never had
to investigate himself,
has never had the instinct
to turn a mirror into a person.
They are whisper-fighting down
a street when Melissa receives an e-mail.

Dear Ms. Melissa Lozada-Oliva

Various sources have informed me that you brought my daughter back to life?????? I am disturbed and chilled at the heinous nature of this act!!!! Who gave you the right????? This isn't your story!!!!!!!!! I watched your videos online—why are you saying all of these things????? The word "Bitches" is not nice!!!!! Does your mother know you are talking this way???? I did like the "My Spanish" one, though I think you could have made it a little nicer!!!! It could maybe even be an anthem!!!! Latinos get the jobs done; are you familiar with the musical *Hamilton*????? To me, it felt sad!!! Your poem, not the musical, which I enjoyed!!!! Are you a sad person???? Why are you so upset???? Your life has been good!!! You aren't even from Texas!!!! Your parents have worked hard!!! You should be nicer to your parents!!! I am suing you for bringing my daughter back to life without my consent!!! I have spent over twenty-five years mourning her!!! Honoring her memory!!! By the way, where is she?????? We spoke on the phone and we haven't heard from her!!!! What have you done?????????? You don't know anything about respect!!! If you had more respect for yourself, you would've gotten a real job like anybody else!!!!! You could've been a dentist!!!!!!!!!!!! It seems like you are not talented enough to have a career on your own, which is your own fault!!!! I am suing you for $70,000!!!! My lawyers will be in contact with you shortly.

Sincerely,
Abraham Quintanilla.

What does it mean when a woman
pulls the trigger?
Some scholars say
that actually, in many ways,
the patriarchy
influenced Selena's murder in all that it
denied Yolanda, which is to say
a reflection.
Which is to say,
whose side are we on here?

Abraham Quintanilla Is Out for My Blood

Once, my sister taught me the washing machine,
that Selena dance move where you swish
your hips around and move in a circle,
like you're a spinning plate of cakes.

It's this way and then that way and like that.
It's Mami's hips, it's my hips, Abuelita's.
Then she said, *Don't tell Mami but I lost my V-Card.*
What? It's not a big deal, don't make me feel paranoid.
I ask her what *paranoid* meant.
She said, *Think about it like, you want to go to the mall*
with your friends but Mami says no but then you go anyway
and the whole time you're paranoid that you're gonna see Mami.

I don't even know why they say lost it.
'Cause what if it was on purpose, you know?
You grab a bag of your favorite clothes
and take the bus downtown in the middle
of the day, leave them on an empty bench
that isn't too covered in pigeon shit
in a sunny enough spot and you don't care
who takes it or tries on your favorite purple skirt
because now it finally belongs to somebody.

I came home with a hickey once and Mami
said, *That's not nice*, a phrase which made me feel
like I was naked in front of many old men while
my mother wept from afar in a glass box.

Walking back to my apartment I swear to God a car is following me.
My therapist asked if I ever feel like someone is following me at night.
A question that offended me, a woman in America.
How much is it me and how much is it America? Where do I start
and where do America's flayed-off limbs end?

Fumbling with my keys, I turn around and I see a man
in his car. Sunglasses on even though it's nighttime.
Eating a pastry in a hurry.

She's opened up something she is unaware of
like when she's all borracha
and says too much at the party
and the information sticks with guests until
they go home and they try to scratch it off
but end up scratching their partner.
There are reports of Selena in pizza shops.
Selena at parties.
Selena signing on to another record deal.
A remembrance tour.
The evil Melissa points to the mirror
and Melissa sees herself old, balding,
forgotten.

Yolanda Saldivar Gets Away With It

Suddenly, there is a hole in the bars.
They melt inward.
I glide my hand through them.
The security guard makes her morning rounds and I clamp her boca
shut with my hand. I cradle the gun to her head and demand
she undress. She nods and begins to unbutton. Her belly fans
over her panties the same way mine does and blue veins sprout
across her corn-flour thighs. Her breasts hang
like two arms of a forgotten sweater.

She's got dyed-black hair that thins at the top in a perfect circle.
In another life, we could be primas.
In this life, one of us
has to die.

I slip into the security guard's blue uniform, I two-step over her body
and the blood spreading around her head. I stash the gun in my pants.
I stop at the water fountain. I sip.   I'm feeling cocky.
                                    I wipe my mouth.
                                    I take my time.
I swing my new baton and whistle.

Blood dries on my face; a small, rusty sun. This uniform is itchy now.
I'm already tired of this role. But I keep swinging. I'm whistling. I'm
humming a song now.

I do not look back.

I whistle into the glaring daylight. I take a right into the parking lot. I take the dead guard's keys and point at cars until one lights up and beeps for me. I enter her basic-white sedan. I turn on the gas.

No one will ask me where I'm going.
No one will ask me who I'm going to be.

Yolanda knocks
on her door
in the middle of the night.
It is a rapid knock,
the kind of heartbeats.
There is a rhythm to it,
a code. She has
no time to process.
Of course she nods her head.
Of course she opens the door
for her wider, softly,
so no one can hear the hinge creak.
Of course
she comes inside.

In Which I Answer All of the Questions from My Imaginary and Very Important Interview of the Future

Well, what is so crazy is that I've practiced this in the mirror before. In fact, I've practiced saying, "I've practiced this in the mirror before." Oh, I could go on and on. When I was a little girl I would give my whole family ticket stubs to see my show, which was, I don't know, this dance I had choreographed to Britney Spears's "Lucky." I had this little dance and I was so ready for everybody to watch it. But I don't remember anybody watching it. What I remember instead is walking into the living room playing the song from the tape I recorded from the radio and my whole family sitting down looking at a camera set up in front of them. They are saying, "We are taking a picture, sit down." I sit down on the seat of the couch. It squeaks because it's wrapped in plastic. We are there for hours and hours. They are sitting and smiling but it's impossible for me. I am restless. I am fidgety. I want to get out of here. I get up and walk over to the camera. I face them. I wave. Their image shows up on a TV screen. There they are, my whole family. I wave at the screen. I say, "Everybody, hello!" Then my mother tells me to sit back down.

El Chisme According to Others:
Yolanda at the Gay Bar

Debbie, 37

Yeah, I recognized her. Said her name was Jessica, but I knew
who she was. Why didn't I call the police? I had empathy. Ever
heard of it? Also for a while I thought she was a police officer.
Uniform and everything. Look, it was a busy night and she was
pretty quiet. Kept downing bourbons. Had a notepad and a pen.
Seemed like some kind of romantic writer, we get a lot of those.
I asked her what she was writing and she covered up her
notepad all defensive, like I just caught her writing in her
diary. She told me, "My story." I was like, right on, okay. Write
your story. Then she started talking to this regular, but then
they started fighting. I try not to pay too much attention. She
left behind her notepad. Just had a bunch of flowers all over it.
All these squiggles. All these arrows pointing nowhere.

Catrina, 22

I came up to her because she seemed lonely. Reminded me of
my tía. I feel sad around old single lesbians, but also I feel a
little in awe of them. Anyway, I brought this up to her, which I
admit might have been insensitive, but I was just looking for
advice, I guess, and she got super defensive, talking bout how
she isn't a lesbian, how that's disgusting, how that's a sin, and I
was like, okay, so why did you come here? She couldn't answer
me. She looked back down at her drink. I made to leave, and I
thought I heard her say, "Don't go."

PART III

YO SE PERDER

Hello again,
querido reader.
Have you ever
remembered an event
differently just so
you didn't have to
change your behavior?
Have you ever listened
to a story and thought,
this person is lying?
Melissa knows the story,
but she's changing
the story.
She inserted herself
and now she can't get
herself out. Some
parts of her feel
asleep, and what if
she never feels them
again fully, just
that tingly,
rained-on feeling?

Yolanda Tells Me

I think about her every day.
The way she smelled—
she was a girl who
smelled good and therefore made me
feel like I stunk, but I think I loved that.
Every other exhale was a laugh,
but always a laugh that was with you,
like she understood what I meant
by all of that saying-nothing,
what my Sunday mornings sounded like,
what the rosaries hanging on my dashboard were for.
It always felt like us against the world.
You must believe me, Melissa.
I am a woman weak
with want and *kill* is such a strong word.
The gun? I bought the gun to protect
myself. Her father, he . . . well,
you don't need to know these things.
Just know that I needed something
to cradle at the time. Just know that
it was the only thing I felt
I was allowed to touch.

Yolanda Tells Me What Happened that Night

I knew something that she didn't want people to know.
No, I will not tell you.
A secret is a secret.
I will take that to my grave.
That's what friends are for.
She fired me.
So I was stealing money.
So I needed to send some to
my mother back home and she wouldn't let me.
There was a misunderstanding. She came to visit me
in my motel.
I was pissed. I put the gun to my head.
She wanted to be friends but I'm a stubborn woman.
I had my dignity.
I said, "If you don't leave right now, I'll kill myself, Selena."
Maybe that was dramatic of me. I have a way of
leading with my feelings.
She said, "No, Mom. Don't do that."
She called me Mom.
She turned around.
I said "Wait." I told her, "Don't go."
I thought the gun was off.

March 31, 1995

This is how my mother tells it. I was three years old and she was taking my tío and me through customs in Guatemala. Because I had the privilege of having my first cries in an American hospital and because my mother is white even in her own country, she could tote me worry-free back and forth from the country she chose and the country she left. She was doing my dad a favor, one of many that she would love to count on drunk fingers when I was just trying to go to bed. She had her brother have a guy who owed him a favor make a fake passport, that looked as real as it could have looked, given the circumstances. My tío spent months mustached and skinny in Guatemala, distilling the song in his Colombian accent with my mother's family's alcohol.

I was old enough to walk then, for her to pinch when I wasn't fast enough, spank me when I was making too much noise.

At the airport, the TV screens kept showing the same red Jeep, the same footage of a young woman who, when she smiled, seemed like her eyes were staring into the sun. Tío didn't know who she was or why so many people around them were crying and so my mother did the work of filling him in, under her breath.

No one would believe he was Guatemalan if he didn't love Selena. Or so she tells me on our way to my sister's house, where her husband is riding his mower and taking in that fresh, nostalgic smell of death. My mother did not trust my tío to say the right thing, so she talked for him. "This one is devastated," she told a stranger, who covered her own mouth, shook her head at the screen. "He was so in love with her." I read somewhere once, as we all do, that your earliest memories aren't reliable. The way we tell stories and the way we remember what really happened drive together somewhere and they fight over the directions and the place you end up is not better than before, but anyway, you're there. So, where was I, where was she, where were we, when they reached customs and the officer looked too hard at my tío's passport, then back at his face, then back at the passport, then back at the bead of sweat dancing down his face? My mother's instincts kicked in. She has told me this story before.

In some versions of this story, she pinches me until I wail.

In others, she whispers, "Cry, Melissa, cry."

In this one, I get myself ready.

In this one, I take a deep breath.

I scrunch up my face and fat tears gather in my eyes and my little brown face turns into the color of a sweet little onion.

In this one I know, I know, I know exactly what I'm doing.

Buenas noches.
The other year you
stopped eating
meat because you said
violence wasn't necessary for survival.
The other day you asked
to be choked during sex
because you needed to
feel loved more severely.
The other day you ignored
the news because it was
"too much for you."
If you are safe can you
even feel alive?
In the end,
what do we all deserve?
Quickly, a flashback
to Halloween
2016.

My Lover Shows Me His Gun Collection

It is Halloween 2016 and we are two weeks away from
everyone talking about the world being on fire.
Jacki is dressed up as a vampire,
but you can only tell if she smiles. Julia is Nancy
Kerrigan but doesn't want to make her knee bloody
because that was corny so instead she is just the ice dancer
before the scream.

I am Mia Wallace and I am trying too hard.

My lover doesn't dress up as anybody because he didn't have time.
Usually, he dresses up as a woman.
Not a specific woman, just a woman.
That's the only joke.

I find him outside smoking.

He looks at me in my black wig and my fake bloody nose and says,
　　Meli, it's you.
I look down at my feet, thought, *Meli, it's you.*
I look out the window of his car, *Meli, it's you.*
I look at the ceiling as he took off my costume in a hurry, with a hunger.
　　It's you.

The next morning he lays his guns out on the bed like dress socks.
He is very excited.
How did I get here?

We were just drinking orange juice.
We were just talking about music.
He hands me the cowboy pistol, and I'm already forming
the story I'll tell my friends later,
the ones I ditched the night before,
when we were all dressed up as women from movies.

He tells me the first rule of gun safety is to point
to the safest spot in the room and there's a baby
downstairs and us right here so the best place
to point is up.

The gun isn't loaded so there's nothing to worry about.
Maybe I've just got to hold it in my hand,
the way I kiss people at parties
like I'm never gonna be this tight and young again,
like I know one day someone's gonna take me out back.

Why doesn't everything end
with something loud that shakes the room?
Boom-boom, it's over, bye-bye, I don't see you anymore.
Boom-boom, the world ends, we gather our essentials, put on our good
     boots,
pack into our cars and head west.

I think I'm bringing my own end.
I'm making everything happen.
I'm moving the air around me
until I'm someone he can choose.

I'm pointing up, to the place where I can't get hurt and I'm pulling
    on the trigger
and there is barely a noise, there is a sound
that could've been
the absentminded click
of the tongue while searching through an e-mail,
the snapping of fingers during a halfhearted
dance at the end of the night,
the sigh that escapes when
you light a match
and it fails to strike.

"If you are here," she asks
Yolanda,
"Then where
is the Yolanda in jail?"
Yolanda shifts
in the room.
The floors creak.
The curtains rustle.
"There can
only be one
of me,"
Yolanda says.

Remember that Yolanda Was a Little Girl Once

She was staring out the window.
She was playing tic-tac-toe.
She was burning spiders with a magnifying glass.
She was straddling a pillow at night.
It was active sitting.
It was imaginative resting.
Closing her eyes, she was trying to think of the right things:
      the sweat on Mr. Martinez's mustache,
      the bulge in the next-door neighbor's shorts.

(In the next room, her mother was crying about bills and about debt and
about family far away.)

She was opening her eyes. She was thinking of
        the blond hairs on Ms. London's wrist
        the golden cross
        how it looks like someone took a glitter pen
and drew it on there,
the phrase: *I believe in you.*

She was dreaming of
tracing her fingers on that honey neck
of yanking whatever God had put there
she was rubbing
the chain
all over her own neck and face,

and that stage between her legs.
She was feeling herself
start to glow.

What If Reclaimed the Woman

who framed her own murder
to get her husband's life insurance,
chopped up her father and stepmother
to protect her lesbian lover,
strangled the girls her mother loved more
and pulled out all their teeth,
put arsenic in the family dinner
and watched all their heads drop,
seduced and murdered her professor
then framed him for suicide,
rescued her favorite author
then chopped off his legs
because he killed her favorite character,
the woman who
held up the gun she bought for protection,
under her own name,
the woman who pointed at
a long, arched back,
coated with black, shiny
hair and said, "Wait,
don't go."

Yolanda asks
what is happening?
Melissa is like
"What do you
mean?"
Yolanda's like,
"It's like I can see you,
but I can't see you."
Melissa looks down at her hands
and they are not there.
Somewhere from the mirror
there is snickering.

Will We Ever Stop Crying About the Dead Star

and all the ways we find them in our hairbrush or
the screens that light up our nine-to-five eyes.
Will we ever stop crying about the dead star,
the one who wrote the song we put eyeliner on to,
the one who we play in the house when there's nothing else
to say to our families, a car game that happens outside of the car,
the feeling of steadily leaving this place but still remaining inside of it.
We say we miss them but we don't mean them.
We mean the autumn we discovered them,
when we had our headphones in and felt like we were
a movie. We mean the way the breeze felt on our skin that day,
while we walked toward our best friend's house.
We mean words put to music that belong
on the refrigerator of our hearts,
a magnet that holds up a picture of our nephews.
We mean a history that was never written for us,
those words that found themselves in our mouths
and danced out so easily.
The words we whispered
to the person we danced with while
looking at the ring on our fingers.
We mean the person they played who felt like
our uncle.
We mean the lines written by a bitter writer
and said so preciously by the performer,
who was able to make the sentiments

into mirrors they held up to us—
we mean our very own precious identity,
turned into a dust and packaged into a pill
we can swallow.
Another one died today and the world felt
darker because we were left with ourselves.
How can I stop crying about the dead star
when I am slowly smoking away in a room?
I am desperate to give everything meaning,
including myself.
I am trying to make this universal.
I am trying to include You.
Once, You told me that You've felt that way before.
You've sat on my bench and You've looked up at the stars,
You've thought: nothing matters, why am I here,
You've thought: I haven't made anything worthwhile and why would
    I try?
But then, You told me, I've gotten cold and I've gone inside.
I've turned on the stove. I've waited for the water to be ready.
I've made myself something to eat.

There were dead celebrities everywhere,
which means everywhere, holes are getting
larger.
Obviously, it was time to make a profit.
It sold out within minutes.
It was sponsored by Instagram
and Facebook.
They have control over
the algorithm, we guess.
Everyone you've ever missed
in one place: Barclays Center.
One night only.
Melissa hates it there.
She walks past the line.
Crumpled printout tickets.
Phones out.
A Telemundo anchor
interviewing a fan in tears.

Dead Celebrity Prom

Here, the audience almost wishes for blood.
For camp, arms waving
off and hastily fastened back on.

        The body breaking and, with a few snaps,
        shuffling itself together again.

They want coordinated dances, hands creeping
to the beat back to their owner.

              But here, there's none of that.

No rekindled romances or feuds.

        No wine spilling out of the hole in Elliott
        Smith's chest.

No flirting between Jimi Hendrix and Amy Winehouse.

Amy is in the center of the dance floor,
arms wrapped around herself.
        But so is everyone.
        There is a general sway, but no music.

Watching Michael there is a sick feeling.
The King is Back but no one wants to talk
about how watching the King is like

watching a video of an
impersonator of the King
                    in a basement
                    with a bad connection.
Prince is here.
That's pretty cool.

              Everyone had to check their bags,
              even though you can't kill the dead twice.
              Outside, there are protestors.
              It's a scam. It's the government.
              It's a promotion for Bieber's new music video.

The air wishes it were metallic.

              After an hour, people start to leave.
              Someone says, "That was so crazy!"
              Another says, "I'll never forget this!"

If they stayed the whole time,
they'd notice the glitching,
the way the dead musicians
gathered in the center,
holding hands.

How they opened their mouths.
How something rang out of them,
like a collective roar
or a feral call to the beyond,
or the sound of many hands
slapping themselves together
until they are raw.

What is happening with
the dead?
Is she the only one who
heard it?
Something big is coming
and it's all her fault.
She takes herself to the bar.
On the screen, Selena's image.
Cameras and microphones all around her.
Melissa feels herself leaving again.
She goes to grab her drink
and her hand isn't there.
Could it be that the realer Selena
becomes, the more Melissa disappears?
The cup does not move
as much as she tries to hold it.
Maybe the cup does not want
to be held.

You and Me Don't Talk Anymore

The beginning,

I don't remember.

a moment of mania, dreamy but unhealthy.

What I said the first night.

Full-throttle and reckless.

I was probably embarrassing.

I wanted to know what would happen next but

But anyway, I was brave.

I am obsessed with crystallizing the past.

I am a moment-to-moment man.

Like a new puppy,

You always rush,

love reminds us that we will die.

chasing what you thought was better.

I tried to sing a song drenched in what

I tried to find you in the decades

whatever you thought of me. But

you drowned yourself in.

you do not see me the way that I want.

You twist my words for your poems.

What I wanted was to explode like a star,

I never said "Time wasn't real."

seeping out space junk from my nostrils.

Time is relative,

You can't understand this wormhole I am.

you aren't spending it with me,

There's probably somebody better,

and that feels very lonely.

I've seen the girl at the coffee shops,

I've seen the girl with a straight face.

  Her sense of humor is

dull spoon with take-out. Come back, clog my

  haunted sink. Bring back your

refined-sugar pop song. Don't

  worry. She's nothing like

without hang-ups and ghosts following her.

She doesn't talk about herself.

A practical, compostable

heart. I'll slam the gas-guzzler shut, wish at the

light pollution. Please, it's better for the long

run. I'm not meant for

the certainty, the calendar of

  you.

She thinks she's found a solution
to the celebrities and herself
disappearing. She tries to make
a deal with the she who hovers above
her at night.
"Take my you," she says.
"we've been fighting a lot
and maybe it's better if I just
put a pin in this. Start over."
When she wakes up in the morning,
the you has been replaced
with a monster man.
Everything smells
like the ocean.
The new You has eaten her cat.
She mourns her cat.
But, as usual, she tries to
make the best of the situation.

Poem for Fucking a Fish

My towering green miracle.
My slimy, socially inept monster.
My scaly codependent amphibian.
My lover made of moss, rising from the waters,
brushing tiny shrimp off Your shoulders.

You're so cute today!
You're so sexy!
Let's go for a walk.

Take my hand and don't hold on too tight
because the last time it left a little bruise.
Not a big deal, just a little one!
Love You :)

I have an idea! Let's take the scenic route and then fuck on a bench.
Okay, You're very shy. Okay. That's fine. We don't have to
do that today. We can just talk.
I love daytime dates!

Who needs a drink. I don't, ha.
You're right it is too hot. You're right, the last time
we went dancing people couldn't stop staring at us because I had You
    dressed up as a
grandmother and put a little scarf around Your head and everyone
    was like, "Why does Your

grandmother have scales? Why are You dutty wining with Your
  grandmother?"
That was a lot for us. Do You want me
to pick You up something from the store?
I know You love Go-Gurt and that's hard to find these days, but
I can go and I can look for You.
You're not hungry?

I actually don't ever know what You're trying to say
because of the inherent difference in the way our mouths move.
Mine moves up and down and Yours is like, a blinding ray of light.
We can just sit here.
This is all I need.
You are so cold but it makes me feel warmer?
You are so green and it makes me blush. When I look at You, my hymen
  grows back.

Hymens aren't even real.
Neither are You.
Hold me.

Push the hair back from my ear.
Put Your mouth-hole to my brow.
How You make the blood run to my cheeks.
How You make my heart roll down a grassy knoll
in a day that never ends.

I wish I could watch a video of us
watching a video of us.
Your butt is so cute I could bite it.

Your laugh is so adorable I could
lock it in the basement and visit it on evenings and weekends.

I'll adjust all of the furniture in my house so You can sit in it and dream
of being somewhere else.
I'll kill neighborhood animals and store them in the freezer to keep Your
blood sugar balanced.

I'll put salt and mysterious green formula into Your bathwater every day
so the air won't drown You.

My ocean with legs.
My oak tree with a dick.
My horny haunted house.
Oh,
I could sing about You.

Yolanda stays in her apartment
and sleeps on her bed.
They talk late into the night.
They bond.
Melissa sleeps on the floor.
She is too polite.
The new you sleeps in the bathtub.
Why has it come to this?
She misses you so much.
She comes home one day and finds Yolanda
talking to the mirror. She is laughing
back and forth with it. But maybe Melissa
made that up. Maybe Yolanda is just looking
at her reflection as a mole threatens
to grow bigger.

I Made You a Playlist to Get the Real You Back Even Though Real You Doesn't Listen to the Lyrics

1.

My parents' song is "Que Tontos Que Locos," a bachata about two lovers who keep seeing other people but really just want each other. How stupid we are, how crazy. That's not my parents' story but the rhythm attached itself to it anyway, like when a cat sinks into your legs in the middle of the night, or a leaf settles into your hair and you don't notice until someone looks at you hard enough and says, "Can I get that?" and then, for a moment, you are touching.

2.

When I look at You, a song gets stuck in my head.

3.

Our bodies are not the same
as they were ten years ago because cells divide
and science, whatever, yada yada.
The only parts of us that remain the same are the hair in our ears.
I learned this from a movie. Does it matter which one it is?
They bend and wither over time because they're the only ones we've got.
Obviously, we are cruel. We turn the volume all the way up so that the
song takes over the air around us, makes it so there is no place we've left
behind or a place to get to, there's just the steady, blaring in-between
that lulls us to sleep.

4.

I pull on the hairs on your arm.
I wonder if they can hear me.

5.

Olivia, who is sensitive, can't listen to certain songs
because they bring her to certain places and then, all of a sudden,
her phone dies so she has no way of getting back home
without walking through the town, asking a local for directions and in turn
making small talk with the local, stopping in a bodega to buy a bottle
of water, getting distracted by a father and his son skipping cracks in the
    sidewalk,
catching her reflection in the mirror of a used electronics store, thinking,
"I didn't look this way when you used to love me."

6.

Puloma is gonna get married one day and I'm going to slow dance
with her to "A Better Son/Daughter" at her wedding
and her husband will be watching and he won't know
any of the words.

7.

Is it masturbatory to think I am going to be the song
you can't remember the name of?
That You'll tell the person next to You

(who is like me except maybe cut in half and bleached
and doesn't care about social media so she only takes pictures
of trails and bugs), "It goes like ba-ba-ba" or maybe it's "Da-da
-da-da" and she doesn't know what you're saying and takes out
her phone to check and the ba-ba-ba and the da-da-da-da is stuck
in your head for the rest of the day and also Your life?

8.

In the dark, Mariajose plays me three different versions of "Tennessee Whiskey."
We can be so honest with each other but never actually
do anything about it. We say we hate
country songs to separate ourselves from whiteness
but what's the difference between a country
song and a ranchera, anyway?
There are men and guitars and horses nearby,
there is inherited land that stretches for miles,
there are alcoholic sweat stains in the shape of a couch,
there is a sun that sets just for us.

9.

Stephanie sings "Hero" by Mariah Carey
at the Miss Teen New England contest in Connecticut.
We spend all day looking for a karaoke version.
We go to RadioShack.
We go to Best Buy.
We go to Newbury Comics.
The best they can do is lower the vocals

so Mariah's voice is a little ghost
around my sister's.
She gets third place.
We keep the trophies in the kitchen, behind glass.

10.

Actually, the first impression made to infants isn't sight but sound.
It seeps through the belly and gets into the amniotic fluid. You probably
already know this. Mami always said I was smart because she put Mozart
on her belly. Maybe Mozart was the first man to get stuck in my head,
the first song I thought was only mine.

11.

It could feel like a knife slicing into the cheese of my brain,
or a cash register violently opening and closing, a restless alarm lover that
    doesn't want me
to sleep. How to get rid of an earworm? The world-
wide internet suggests
chewing gum or having a conversation
or listening to the song all the way through,
or picturing the song ending,
for closure.

12.

Abuelita wants them to play Vicente Fernández
at her and Mariano's wedding in the hospital chapel,

but all they have is the in-house music therapist
on his flute. At the funeral, we bury Mariano's ashes with a corona
as his sister sings a song in Spanish. I don't remember the name of the
　　song now,
and two minutes later, she did not remember that he was dead.

　　13.

Chris blasting Bomb the Music Industry! to stay awake
on the New Jersey Turnpike, Samuel handing me the aux cord
asking what do I mean I don't know "Bones" by the Killers? Jess touching
my leg on the highway and saying that this Best Coast song isn't about Love
it's about being an addict, Connor not saying anything
when I play "Yellow Eyes" on the Tobin Bridge.
Will sending me a recording of him singing Mitski
and not telling me his feelings were hurt when I didn't respond.
Jon singing the bridge of
"Say It Ain't So" in the car with Rae
at a stoplight at the top of his young lungs before the song
was a meme or a memorial. All of my lovers, all of my friends.
There is no song that belongs just to us.

　　14.

I wear the songs out.
I leave them out in the sun.
I forget to feed them.
I throw them in my backpack.
I get on my bike.

They rattle inside where they get scratched up
by my keys, my chargers, my pens, everything
I think I need to carry
with me as I make my way to You.

She is losing herself
and scrolling.
She is on Twitter
and reading an
interview with
Selena.

Are you worried about reports of Yolanda Saldivar being on the loose?

No offense, sweetie, but it's time to get cancelled for *good*! Made my family suffer so much. She deserves to be punished and that's on periodt.

Tell me about the new Selena doll

I made the new Selena doll because representation matters. Think about it. You grow up only playing with dolls for white girls, well guess what? Every girl deserves to hold a doll that looks just like her. Now, they finally can. We cannot truly see ourselves until we really see ourselves, as Audre Lorde once said. You can buy them in most record shops for $29.99. Use the discount code SELENAFOREVER to get 5% off.

And what about the young woman who brought you back to life, Melissa Losado-Oliviiana

I don't know who that is! No comment.

We Cry About It Together

We cry about it. She left us.

She doesn't care about us.

We might as well be dead, but more importantly,

she might as well be dead.

She had the selfish gene and it mutated.

It caught onto us. It put knives in our hands.

We make a pit outside. We dance around it and laugh.

I pull my head back and cackle. It comes

out of me like thunderclap.

I feel a rush of something toward Yolanda,

this woman who found me.

You scratch at the window with your green claw.

I embrace Yolanda.

Something enters me.

I look down at my stomach.

Blood gushing. My hands, covered

in myself. I scream.

She peels me with expert ease.

You roar from inside.

My skin falls at my feet.

I am pulsing and red and then invisible

Yolanda runs away with my flesh husk. I watch my face

bounce against her hip.

Yolanda Leaves a Note

You think every story is about you.

I understand.

When you are denied yourself you must insert yourself.

You use the tools around you and you make a mess.

You fuck up the drywall.

There's dust so tiny that it gets into your lungs.

It kills you eventually.

But wasn't that better than trying to find yourself

in the junkyard of Latinidad? Picking up old

teacups and swearing that you love this cup so much

that it changed your life already, that you'll sip from it forever?

You will talk breathlessly about your latest fixation

and your friends will shake their legs, wonder when

they can finally check their phones.

And who are your friends, do you think?

And do you believe you are loved?

Tell me, is every party you throw

just to see who would show up at your funeral?

I know; you think I am extreme.

You think I am an accelerationist.

You think I am imbalanced.

You think I need help.

But please,

tell me the name of the person you would die for.

Tell me about your precious career.

Tell me about confessional poetry.

Tell me about how you've turned
everyone you've ever met into a poem.
You can't immortalize everybody.
You can't just bring people back to life.
I killed her, okay.
I killed her just to see myself better.
But what are you doing here,
with your eyes?

She finds the You
shot through the head
or what she thinks is the head—
she can't really tell.
So long, monster lover.
She feels relieved but sad,
like when a successful
person is hotter than her
or like when her phone dies.
Pero, he was kind of cute, though!
Muscular.
Is it betrayal
if she should have just
known better?
Que tonta, honestly.
Yolanda?
Yolandaaaaa!
Yolanda is gone.

El Chisme According to Others:
Where Is Selena?

Devin, 22

She seemed really busy when I was asking her those questions.
An assistant was doing her hair up and another one was
painting her nails. She was transfixed by the mirror. I looked
in the mirror to see what she was seeing but saw just the four
of us. She had her eyes narrowed. I could tell something was
wrong. This was gonna serve as a really good clip (it's really
exhausting being a sex and love writer) but I feel like she didn't
really *give me* anything. And this is weird but after she would
say something I thought I could hear a click, like it was a
recording? I don't know if I'm being problematic. There's a lot of
new language lately about how to talk about the dead, so I'm
still learning. But . . . yeah. The click. And in the middle of the
interview, she just got up and left. No explanation. Just walked
away from us.

Stacy, 36

I dropped my kids off with my mom. I wasn't gonna miss this.
Concert of . . . my life. I showed up there wearing my best
Selena. Went by myself. It was a treat-myself. It was for my
birthday. I get there. It's packed. I had taken my anxiety
medication and everything. Then, two hours go by. Nothing.
She doesn't show up. I sit down. My feet are tired. I'm
disappointed.

Mikey, 45

She started comin' in about a month ago. She looked kinda
funny. Something about how when I looked at her I could also
hear her. Or I had this feeling that's the same feeling when you
go under the tunnel and the radio goes out? Or when there was
still dial-up and you'd wait in front of your piece-a-crap desktop
to get connected? That's how it was to look at her. I chalked it
up to lack of sleep. Got a four-month-old that's been keeping me
up all night. So I say to her, you know, what can I get for you,
miss? She says, "I could eat a whole pepperoni pizza by myself."
I go ahead and I make her a nice pie. Ask her for $13, standard,
kind of a deal in the city, to be honest with you. She didn't
know how to use the chip thing so I asked her if she had Apple
Pay and she looked at me all confused. She didn't sign. Few
days later I started seein' stuff on the news. Reports of Dead
Pop Star Selena in New York City. Then there were others.
Elvis. Michael Jackson. I said to my wife, I said, "Honey, is the
world ending?" I don't know what's gonna happen next. Is there
gonna be some kind of reckoning? Should we start goin' to
church again? Should I reconnect with my brother? We're
always very polite to her. How's it goin', Selena? How was your
weekend, Selena? We ask her if she wants the usual. The ones
who haven't seen her yet, the ones who are just here for the
summer, they get a little scared. They're just kids. But they've
heard the stories. It's all true. Whole thing is pretty freaky to
me, but ya know? I want to treat her like a normal person.
What's the difference between her and me, know what I'm
talkin' about? At the end of the day she's just a girl who loves
pizza. Haven't seen her for a while now, actually.

PART IV

COMO ME DUELE

Yolanda Wears Melissa's Skin into Selena's Hotel Room

I will be the name you pass around the house on your good china.

I will be the clap before the lights go off.

I'll have assistants.

I'll say to them, "What's the update on the 41C?"

I will have codes like "41C."

I will take baths and dry off with wads of cash.

I will have sex and then more sex.

I'll order food with confidence.

I'll never be behind bars again.

I will run up the stairs then down the stairs

then down the stairs.

I will make it to this hotel room, where

I know where she is.

I want to show her my new body.

I want her to know that it's me,

that it's really been me,

after all this time.

She'll know.

She'll know right away.

I sneak my way into the lobby.

I ask the right questions.

I feel giddy in my new skin.

I stretch it just for good measure.

I get a key card.

I knock on the door.

I slip the key in with pleasure.
I say, "Surprise! It is me."
But the room is empty.
Where is she?

Hellraiser

My ID is expired but maybe in the next life I'll give my body to science.
My heart would've given a hopeful ballerina another forty years of hating
    herself
or a greedy politician another thirty years of covering himself up.

I walk down the street in a trench coat and sunglasses.
I scream when I put on the clothes.
I am slimy, raw, and pulsing.
I am a clit with the hood pushed back,
hitting the hot water in the shower.
I am a hangnail all over.
I am trying to act normal.
A child sees me slide my
MetroCard and gasps at my hand,
which is exposed like
a photo of two lovers caught in a seedy hotel room
or an ATM receipt outside the scene of a crime
or a reblogged Tumblr post from 2012 with racist epithets
or an essay found on a desktop about why *Girls* is actually a really good
    show.

It hurts to touch anything but maybe in a few days
all I will know is the hurt
and how it defines me.
I'll crawl into the shape of the pain and
make my home there.

I'll invite my friends over and they'll make excuses to leave.
I'll say, "It's so good to see you, tell me all about California!"
Then I'll go to touch them and they'll flinch,
and they'll feel ashamed that they flinch,
sad about this instinct to be afraid of me.
They'll wash the pink goo that came from me off later, in
the bathrooms they keep tidy.

There's a gust of wind and my hat blows off on the train's platform.
My glasses, too. My trench coat blows against me, pathetically.
I see people steal glances and then look down in fear.
My lonely and obvious insides screaming.
The world hearing them but refusing to look up.

The playlist,
while well-meaning,
never got to the You
or it did but could only be played
backward with unintentional
shout-outs to Satan.
She knows what she must do.
In many ways, she has been
waiting for this her whole life
and so have we.
She has to go to hell now
and rescue the You *from damnation,*
and she must kill Selena
for the second time and retrieve
her skin.
But how to do that?
Better to put it off.
Procrastinate and go
to karaoke.

Killing Time at Karaoke

Has everything I've ever done
been just an imitation of something else?
I'll never be remembered, I'll always
sabotage any romance I ever have
because of some warped thing inside
of me that I've never contended with,
inherited from the colonizer and the colonized.
I don't know, I think I read that somewhere.
In many ways I am a poser and a loser and a jerk.
Why did I do this? Why did I ever do anything?

I'm at karaoke taking sips from a stranger's
drink because the bartender refuses to look at me.
I leave remnants of myself on the glass and try to
wipe it off with my trench coat.
I feel overcast. Like I'm about to burst.
Every Thursday at midnight
the KJ chooses a name
from the bucket and that person gets
to sing "Dancing on My Own."
I never get picked. He turns off
the lights and takes out his
cell phone and makes a strobe light
by putting his hand in front of it
and moving it up and down.

I never get picked except for this time.
My name echoes throughout the room
and this time, people are looking at me,
smiling empathetically, like I'm some kind of burn
      victim.
They are clapping. They are woo-ing.
I'm surrounded by so many friends.
I get up on stage. The music begins.
And then. Poof. It's the same room but it's
not the same room. The KJ has been
replaced by the She.

She's gotten ahold of the audio system.
The speakers blast my insecurities
in my mother's voice. I feel hungover.
I understand that I am in hell.
I ask her, *What do you want.*
What do you really really want?
and she begins to duplicate.

      I'm staring at myself
      surrounded by myself.
      I'm trapped in a room
      with me. Somewhere
      among all of me
      I can hear
      Selena singing.

She pushes past herself,
trying to concentrate
on her voice.
Suddenly, she's in a flashing hallway.
All of the Shes *are chasing her*
but only as fast as she can run,
which isn't that fast.
She's in the karaoke
place where she had her quinceañera.
Rooms and rooms of
single karaoke booths.
Places where one can be vulnerable
without being too vulnerable.
She arrives at a front desk and
there is her precious You.
She can't believe it.
It's really You.
But he is busy now.
All dial-up and mixed signals.
But then, oh! The You *disappears*
and she is locked in a room
filled with screens.

Her Funeral Plays on a Loop

on the walls.
Her father throws himself on the casket
over and over again. The cries from her family
echo. They get louder.
The evil me is in the middle of the room.
Her breath smells like cheap wine.
She's wearing a slip and I can see her nipples.
I'm like, OK I kinda look really good?
She is shifting. She is in a wedding dress now.
She is an older woman with a knife in her hand.
Now she is my mother.
My sisters.

My middle school bully.
Now she is Selena, her hips swaying back and forth.
I get closer and closer to her.

A gun appears in my hand.
It's a cowboy gun then
it's a glock
then it's a machine gun
then it's a water gun
then it's a wet fish.
Evil me shifts and shifts until I am inches away from her.
Now she is just Selena.
Selena wearing my headphones.
Selena wearing my jean jacket.

Selena smiling at me.

There are tears in her eyes.

She stops dancing but she does not stop smiling.

Oh, how it hurts me.

I say, *Don't leave me, Selena.*

She says nothing to me.

I say I swear to god I'll do it, Selena!

I point the gun to my head but the gun

is a red rose,

then a rubber chicken, then a real chicken,

then a small white dove flying away.

She will never know

the way Dr. Louis Elkins

described her heart:

A normal heart looks like a fist,

he said to the jury.

Bright pink, or red.

Her veins had collapsed

by the time I had arrived.

Her heart was blue.

I point the gun back at Selena and it's just a gun.

She turns around.

Don't go, I say.

There is no sound.

She's crumpled on the floor.

I kneel beside her.

Her outfits change.

The purple jumpsuit.

The black studded bustier and the newsboy hat.
A classic white blouse tied at the waist and a pair of jeans.
Pajamas.

On the screens, static.
In my ears, deafening dial-up.
Her body is gone, now.
I am left with the wires
and my blood,
the blood that made this.

Oh Selena, it happened again.
and it is my doing.
My fault, my desire
to turn a mirror
into a person.
My own two stupid fists,
punching the air
but still bleeding.

You appear behind me,
Your hand on my shoulder.

Selena Dies a Third Time

I think the most difficult thing is when.
Thank you, it's a real pleasure for us to be.
Taste of honey, little bit of rock.
¿Por que no me corregiste? ¡Sí!
I hate it when y'all say that I'm the
woman because I hate it when y'all are
right. Without you guys, I'm nothing, thank you.
Pizza, double pepperoni.
I had this huge knot in my stomach. I was so nervous.
It's an honor, thank you, a real pleasure.
Que tal amigos. Y me como de todo.
¡Ojala vamos a ver a todos muy pronto!
It was the very first time, it will be the last too.
It's been great. It's been really great.
What's it like? Well, it's like a dream come true.

We Begin to Slow Dance

Who put on our song?
It starts to snow.
The skin on my hands
has returned but it
keeps turning.
Spots scatter across.
More, now.
Veins appear, plump and purple.

The ends of my hair touch my ass
the way I've always wanted them to.
the way they could've
had I just been more patient,
had I spent less time in front
of mirrors, trying to change
immediately.

But the hair is white, now.
Thin. It keeps stretching
past my ankles. I hear it
swishing on the floor.

I know that if I reached for
my head I would
find the flabby coolness
of my scalp.
I move

my weathered hands
to your chest.
I move my hands to your neck.
where I feel a picture of us
from last summer.

You smell like stolen wifi and the snow
makes your eyelashes spark.

You ask me if I'd like to sing and I hear it
through your skin.

There Is Only One Way Out

It's midnight at the karaoke bar. But I'm thinking it always is. Here, we have to pay with secrets. I've told you everything already so you put in two for me. I try not to think of the secrets nestled in the fishbowl, overlapping each other with their rips and folds.

We look in every room. Sometimes it's Selena singing in the rooms. Sometimes it's me. Sometimes it's Selena and me, sewed together and fighting over the microphones. Sometimes it's You singing with somebody else. I hate that one.

We enter a room together. You are not singing. I must sing for you. There are fifty thousand songs to choose from and I type in the one I know the best. You get up and go to the bathroom in the middle of the song. I'm offended but I keep going. I know I have to keep singing in order to get myself out of here. I know I have to be okay with wherever it is You go. I know I have to be okay with who You want to be. So, I sing. I sing and I sing. I can only hear the music. I have to trust that I know it. That I can hit all of the notes. There is no applause. There is no one else singing along. The Selenas do not come in, impressed with my range. The Evil Me doesn't ridicule me. There really is no reason to be here. What does it matter if no one is watching me? If no one is cheering me on? I close my eyes. I am crying, which is humiliating, but it's not like anyone can see. There are no windows. There are no mirrors. I have no idea what I look like. I have no idea how I sound.

When Selena sang
"como me duele," she meant
us; how it hurts us.
But before that comes the cry.
The ay-ay-ay.
That wail that can only come from
sad drunk men standing outside
of houses, their wives at the window
with their arms folded or women holding
photographs of the sons
who never came back from the war
and children now, being ripped from embraces,
watching their mothers get farther and farther away
from them. Selena cried for us, but first she waited.
There was that pause.
And that space between her and us.
That all-knowing delay?
That space between the stage and the floor?
The buzzing in the air?
The desire, the beckoning?
That is where we want to live.

Yolanda Saldivar Orders a Stack of Pancakes

She asks for more syrup.
The waitress points to the packaged kind on the plate.
Yolanda says *I want the real thing.*
The waitress shakes her head and Yolanda squeezes syrup over her
pancakes. She watches the butter melt,
turn from a solid block
to a shapeless thing that gives up and blends in.
The waitress turns on the TV,
where the same clip of Selena in a gurney
flashes across the screen.
The waitress has her hand on her hip. She squints.
Yolanda waits for her name to appear, her picture.
It doesn't.
The waitress folds napkins into the silverware.
She hums something unnamable to herself.
Yolanda shakes her head.
She cuts them into little triangles.
She takes a bite.

Last Chisme Before We Go

Carmen, 26

I was getting some flowers for my boss. It felt like a Thursday but maybe it was a Tuesday. She wasn't sad or anything; she just wanted to brighten up the office. Air quality in New York, all of that. I got three white roses from Cesar at the flower shop. He was spray painting them white. He saw me spraying and maybe self-consciously he said, "Nobody notices." He asked me about my mother. He was ringing me up when the flowers started getting loud. Déjà vu is when your mind is remembering something as it's happening, right? It usually happens when you're really tired or depressed, I think. The flowers were loud and I felt like I had been there before. Many, many times. As different people, almost. Then the flowers started to shake. I heard a choking sound. A screaming sound. A sound that's like someone chasing after the person they love because they dropped their wallet but that person is already blocks and blocks away and that person has already put her headphones in. My face was wet. Cesar, too. We hugged. We said "Sorry," but we didn't know why. Then I went away.

Junot, 52

I saw her. I did. It was like I peeked inside of a can of Café Bustelo and just found a beating heart spouting out period blood. Like I woke up next to a cat purring beside me and when I reached to pet it, all this human hair came off in my hand and all the human hair was mine. Like I tried to jerk off but my dick was just the edges of paper and it gave me little cuts on my hands. Like I saw a beautiful woman walking down the street, a really beautiful one right, with tits that were laughing at me through her paper-thin shirt and an ass that was fighting out of her jeans and hair that was flapping behind her like a black broken wing and when I went to look behind me there was just a big gaping hole in the air, a wet open mouth whispering or screaming or moaning at me, asking me to come closer and tell her what would come next.

The celebrities are gone now,
gracias a Dios.
No one could handle the drama.
No one knows who brought
them back or how. It fizzes away.
On to the next chisme.
She doesn't text or tweet or take a picture.
Some things are better to let
wilt in your memories, mami.
We wish we could tell her that.
But we think she knows now.

It's not like
the two of them
can go back to the way
that it was.
She didn't manipulate
time.
She brought
the dead back, then
returned them.
But the You?
What are the consequences
for this trade?
Will the You be jet-lagged
from the afterlife?

EPILOGUE

How to tell
the end of
a ghost story
when everything
is haunted anyway?
Adios, querido reader.
Ciao, nuestro amor.
Cuidate, okay?
On to the next disaster.
We will be watching you!
Not to creep
you out or anything.
But, oh, mi vida, we know
you.
We know
you love that.

Yolanda and Selena Don't Talk Anymore

I stopped you just in time.
Now you'll be remembered
They'll never hear me sing.
Most of the time,
I'm a villain
or a lesbian.
Jealousy reveals
a Polaroid of the women I am not
When I called you "Bitch!"
and shot you
what I meant was,
"Love!"
I just didn't want you to go.
In another life,

To dream about love
for all eternity. That's why
death isn't so bad. I like to think I've been pretty
lucky for all of my life.
I'm a saint
who loved too hard, trusted too deeply.
a prayer whispered violently.
a letter stained with fear.
I heard fans cheering. Their hands came together
because they loved me.
My heart was once the shape of
a pink fist before it turns blue.
I was brain dead before I was a headline.
In this dream,

I am someone I can be proud of.

I am a wife and a mother

The face you see in the moon

a woman who says "Yes."

In another life,

I'm marinating steak & when you wanna bite

You want to love me

I let you.

We are on the road going 85

Somewhere far away, I am

playing a tape with only two songs.

on a loop and

My arm is around your shoulders and

I can't stop smiling.

we are wasting time like water,

I am still alive and everyone is watching -

you're breathing

an entire country, singing

in my ear.

It's Selena's Birthday in Salina, Kansas

On the plane I have a dream about
a woman with bright pink lipstick
who says to me, with familiarity,
"I'm glad they recorded our old age."

When we land,
the pilot starts to back all the way up,
fast, like he's racing backward.
I grab the woman's wrist on instinct.

I say, "I'm sorry, that was random,
I was just afraid." She tells me,
"Don't be, look at the flowers outside—
they are the only ones here."

When I wake up,
we are still in the air
and the woman next to me
is different, snoring, older.

In the Beginning

You wiped dust on your kitchen floor
with your hands because you were too impatient
for paper towels. In the beginning, we were all on the floor
at your aunt's house and our friend said,
Do you remember when you came to visit me and the dogs
and you told the dogs, "I love you. I tell animals that and nobody else."
Those dogs are dead now.
Isn't that funny? Isn't that the most hilarious thing?
We avoided our eyes then, afraid of saying
what was there but letting it squirm
around us and sink into the other's cheeks.
In the beginning, we were at the beach,
and it was so unforgivably hot.
We drank water. We jumped in.
I watched your back and you watched
the water fold out before you.
You turned your head around and we made
eye contact as I started to pee and we started
to laugh and if you turn your head upside down
like this, no—this way—the ocean looks like the sky.
If you kiss a dog enough times
they'll stop peeing on the floor.
If I say your name now and you
turn your head and you do not recognize me
then fuck, I don't know.
Then I am dreaming

of you dreaming of me, again.

Then I'll wait here till you're ready and while I'm waiting

I'll make my home here,

in this undefinable space I can try to name and then try to name again

until I give up on names altogether, just let them go through my fingers

like water, like trying to remember the freakiest moments of a nightmare,

but it's too late—I'm already awake and the day is about to start and

I have to set up a bird feeder and propagate more plants today.

I have to hang up signs.

I have to open up the windows.

I have to look far out

to see that line

where the water

becomes air.

ALTERNATE ENDING

Selena Doesn't Die

She just makes more hits. Another bop. Commercials. She stars in a movie with Johnny Depp. There is a flirtation. There are rumors. She takes a hiatus from music after a throat condition. She buys a farm in San Antonio with white horses & her husband. Johnny calls her at 12:47 a.m. every night. She twists a phone cord around her finger. There is giggling. There is a day that Johnny stops calling. Selena tries to distract herself. Selena looks at her sleeping husband & sees a good man. In the evenings they look each other in the eye & one says "Pizza?" & the other says "Pizza!" There are days & days of pizza. Five months go by & still no word from Johnny. Selena cuts her hair on impulse. The locks drop to the bathroom floor, a small, dark, sleeping creature. Selena thinks about selling it but there is freedom in what you decide to throw away. Selena doesn't return her agent's calls. She is heartbroken but can't tell anyone about it. Selena eyes a man at the gas station & one night when her husband is out she invites him over & they fuck in the horse stable. She feels very alive. Her husband comes home & she confesses. He hits her. No. Her husband comes home & she confesses & he thinks about hitting her but the white horses interrupt; they buck & they neigh & they demand to be looked at. No, her husband comes home & she says nothing at all & he kisses her good night. I love you. I love you, too. No, her husband doesn't come back at all. He climbs into his car & the car evaporates. Poof. Good-gone. Selena's belly grows rounder & the days stay the same because she is in a sunny place. Her baby comes. She names her Flor because she's always

Selena Still Isn't Dead

She's inspired again. Flor & Selena sing together at the piano. The hits keep coming. A guest spot on Jimmy Fallon, a song featuring Pit Bull. There is a goldfish then a funeral for the goldfish. Selena teaches Flor how to ride a bike & Flor falls down. Flor gets a scrape on the knee. Selena sings the song about the frog to it & the song scrapes the dirt out of the wound & seals on its own. Selena's father babysits Flor. She runs around in the yard chasing the family cat & the way her hair blows from behind her makes Abraham spooked, in the way that all lineage is a little spooky. A little freaky. A little flash of all the ways things could have been different, but then the moment passes. So long. Bye-bye. He teaches her how to play the drums & while she's really good, she's too distracted by the sun yelling outside, & well, maybe this kid can just be a kid. Abraham spoils her in a way he never spoiled his children. They all point this out. Flor has it easy. Flor jumping on the trampoline all afternoon. Flor making a puppet show out of Abraham's shoes. Flor with hobbies that can't make any money. Who cares. Flor getting taller, now. Flor with budding breasts. Flor lying about where she is. Flor with a pregnancy test banging around in her backpack. Flor's eyes watering with relief when she wakes up to blood swimming down her leg. Flor at a party with C-list celebrities, bored. Flor doing cocaine before she graduates high school. Flor with a DUI. Flor's year off before college. Flor, missing. Flor. Where is Flor. Have you seen her? What did she say when you saw her? Did she seem sad? Did she say anything about me? Flor, if you're seeing this, honey, please come home. Hello? Flor? Is that you, baby? Where have you been? Do you need me to come get you? Just stay there I'll be

Selena Still Has Some Time Left

so she tries to make the most of it. There is a book deal. There are meetings with a ghost writer. There is a happy year of cooking together, of showing up to events on each other's arm. Then it's over. There is someone who catches Flor's eye. Another call from far away: "I'm in love. Mami, I'm in love. I'm afraid about what you're going to say." There is a bride waiting anxiously for her mother's face to appear in the pews. There is a modest party with strangers. There are years with no contact. There is a breast lump in the shape of Texas. There are doctor's visits & second opinions & third & fourth opinions & more bad news. There's a nest of grey hair in the bathroom drain. There is a hospital bed. There is a dramatic reunion. Hands clenched, foreheads pressed together, sweating. Tears. There is something the both of them always needed to hear. There is a notification on our phones. There are shirts for sale at Urban Outfitters, think pieces, vigils, podcasts, face filters. Flor gets a divorce. It was mutual, a slow fade out, the credits rising up like smoke signals. Flor takes vitamins. Flor ignores the white hairs springing out of her scalp. Flor starts a candle business. Coconut wax with red petals settled spontaneously at the bottom in jars she gathered from street corners & the beach. Flor ships the candles all over the country, sometimes the world, with a line from her mother's songs. Nobody knows it's her. She likes that. The candles burn down. The jars get reused for dinner parties or tossed out again, another life over. Flor goes to marches. Flor tweets about assassinating the president. Flor deletes her Twitter. Flor throws her phone into the river. Flor stops gathering jars. Flor sells her bicycle. Flor orders a gin & tonic at the bar because even though she's sober she doesn't believe in absolutes. There is a woman across the bar making eyes at her. The woman lifts up her hand like, "Hey." Flor lifts her hand up like

RESURRECTING SELENA

MY REASONING

Because it is not enough to be seen
Because I need to see
Because I miss her even though I've never met her
Because it had to be me
Because if it wasn't
Then it wouldn't have been
Somebody else

THE METHOD

I'm tired of feedback and I'm addicted to the internet. IF someone else gets involved it would just be too messy. I need flowers, I need a moonlight dance, I need a song to sway to and access to wifi. I do some research. I go down YouTube holes. I come up with my own method.

HOW I BROUGHT SELENA BACK

① I grow out my hair, purchase chunky gold hoops, buy some bright red lipstick that will stain. This is mainly for effect but it can't hurt.

② I sing backward into a recording device and then play the recording device backward

③ I can't tell my friends anything about this because they would think I'm nuts.

⑤ I take out a loan and turn my bedroom into a lab. I take a USB drive full of Selena's images, songs, and interviews and put it into a pot of my period blood. After three weeks pass,

⑥ I sing backward into a recording device and then play the recording device backward.

...to grow at its ends. I set up a table. I draw a figure on the table using lipstick.

6 I spray You in the face because I'm a reactive person.

12 Days go by. Finally, it is midnight and storming. I take the USB out of the pot of period blood and I put it in some soil. I add fertilizer. I've never been good at waiting.

13b You lose me among the trees. I hear You calling my name. I want You to keep chasing me and I don't want You to find out how far I would go to find out the truth of something, to scratch an itch that will tear the whole universe open. I'm sorry about this but I'm not sorry about this. I'm already lighting the candles. I'm drawing a circle in the dirt with salt. I'm taking off my shoes. I'm already feeling the dirt beneath my feet dance.

EXCERPT FROM "DREAMING OF YOU" BY MELISSA LOZADA-OLIVA & ART BY TiFFANY MALLERY

7 There's more to do. I make You up and ask You to quickly think of the name of the girl in elementary school with the prettiest handwriting.

8 I walk into the kitchen, tie a red string around my finger, say this girl's name five times while spraying Fabuloso into the air. You walk in on me and are all "What are you doing?"

10 I run away because I'm a reactive person.

11 I come back because I've thought about what I've done.

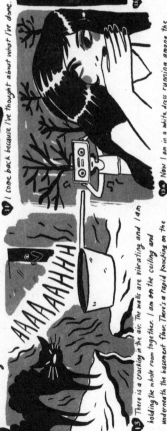

13a Now I am in a white dress running among the trees. You are behind me holding up a jukebox and it's playing something with drums.

AAAAAAHHHH

13 There is a cracking in the air. The walls are vibrating and I am holding the whole room together. I am on the ceiling and underneath the basement floor. There's a rapid knocking on the sliding screen door. A scream coming from the pot. My cat hisses. The lights turn on and off. I am in the closet spying and outside of the closet feeling like I'm being watched. Now it is midnight. I open a girl-shaped door. The knob holding my hand. A cloud of pink is in front of me, rising from the table. The kind of stuff that leaks from attics. I put my hand in and scream.

ACKNOWLEDGMENTS

Thank you to the editors of the following journals, which first published these poems, some in slightly different forms:

"Yolanda & Selena Don't Talk Anymore"—Redivider Journal

"My Lover Shows Me His Gun Collection," "Untitled For Now"—Pigeon Pages

"I'm Not a Virgin But"—Cosmonauts Avenue

"The Future is Lodged Inside of the Female"—Breakbeat Poets: Latinext

"Yolanda Saldivar Gets Away With It," "Hellraiser," "Karaoke Interlude,"—The Poetry Project,

The line "As a star I can only see because it has died," is inspired by a line in Nicole Sealey's "Medical History" in which she says, "And I understand/the stars above me are already dead."

The poem "Resurrecting Selena" is after Terrance Hayes' poem "Instructions For A Séance with Vladimirs"

The poem "I am So Lonely I Grow a New Hymen" is after Sandra Cisneros' poem "I Am So in Love I Grow a New Hymen"

The poem "Will We Ever Stop Crying Over the Dead Star?" is after Olivia Gatwood's poem "Will I Ever Stop Writing About the Dead Girl?"

"Poem For Fucking a Fish" would not be possible without Jamie Loftus' Paste article, "Creatures and the Women Who Want to Fuck Them"

Certain passages from the Chismosas are inspired by theory from Deborah Paredez in her book *Selenidad*, where she speaks about Selena's murder being the product of patriarchy and the way "Como la Flor" is a song about collective cultural pain.

Selena's Sonnets were taken from a compilation of interviews digitized by the Smithsonian's National Museum of American History called "Selena Interview 1994" and parts 1-4 of a Youtube series called "Selena: Funny Diva Moments" uploaded by youtube user Mister Golightly.

The line "a fist the color of a heart before it turns blue" is from the testimony of Dr. Louis Elkins during Yolanda Saldivar's trial.

I want to first thank my family. To Mami & Papi, for giving me the privilege of dreaming. To my big sister Stephanie, who showed me Selena. To my haunted little sister Mariajose, who inspired the freakiness of this book. Thank you Tío Juan for the story. A mi Abuelita, la doña Fransisca Villeda: yo siempre escribo por ti.

Many, many thanks to my phenomenal agent Rachel Kim, for her irreplaceable eye, her encouragement, and her perfectionism. To my editor, Danny Vazquez, all-around cool guy, for advocating for me so much and taking a chance on my freaky book. To the folks at Astra House for giving these poems a home. To Polly Nor for illustrating the coolest cover ever and Richard Oriolo for the amazing design. Thank you. You all made my dreams come true.

I am immensely grateful for my time at NYU. So much love and appreciation to Matthew Rohrer, for when I said that I wanted my thesis to be a rock opera, you said, "hell yeah." I'm so thankful for the guidance of Terrance Hayes, Deborah Landau, Rachel Zucker, Hari Kunzru & Sharon Olds. My cohort was really special, but I especially wanted to shout out Sarina Romero, Kyle Carrero Lopez, and Crystal Valentine. I am forever thankful for our "study group" and this book would not have existed without your good humor and your care. I also have to thank all the teachers who believed in my silly ass over the years: Mr. Finnegan, Mr. Giordano, Mr. Morris, Ms. Dilworth, and Lowry Pei.

Thank you Olivia Gatwood, for being so obsessed with dead girls & dying with me, believing in me so fiercely, and teaching me how to love people better. Puloma Ghosh, my forever-friend, for always looking backward with me & for the notebooks. My love to Delilah, Anna & Leila, my first roommates in New York City. Thank you Lauren & Elizabeth, who put up with Frank. Joey Tepper, who gave me the nightmare tinder bio. Sam Rush, who is canonically the most popular in school. Jessi Rizkallah, who was a protagonist with me after I had a panic attack at Barclay's. Jamie Loftus, who helped me reach the creepiest parts of myself & kiss them on the mouth. Luna Gallegos, who made sense of me being a touring artist while I wrote this book. Ellen Kempner, who, without her songs and without her fierce friendship, some of these poems wouldn't have been possible. Samuel Abotar-Ogoe Jr., who showed me "Bones." Christopher Lee-Rodriguez & Tiffany Mallery, whose union made me believe I had magic powers. Sami Martasian, who gave me slime. Eduardo Rivera, Eduardo Palma & Alejandro Viera, who let me in the band. One day I'll write songs in Spanish. Hieu Minh Nguyen, who made me a better writer and a better friend. Thank you, Tatiana Johnson-Boria, who told me I was ready to go to New York. Jared Gniewek, who turned karaoke into heaven. Will Zhang, who sent me songs & chisme. Thanks to Hannah Rego, who screamed next to me. Suzy Exposito, Don Calva, Hannah Schneider, Melissa Rocha: I hope we can sing together soon. Thank you Porsha Olayiwola & Janae Johnson, who brought me to poetry. Thanks you Jonathan Mendoza, for the help with the very first drafts of the Yolanda poem and for the convos about identity. Thanks to Zoey Walls, Liam, Liz Sher, Nina Jobim, Jazzy D., Rae Jereza, Jess H., Jon S., all of my exes, Topos Book Store, Café Erzulie, Mil Mundos Book Store, Harvard Book Store, and the Ridgewood Public Library. And thank you Ben, for getting stuck in my head. I dreamt about you the most.

One more: Who would I be without Selena Quintanilla-Perez? Thank you. Rest easy, reina.

PHOTO BY BENJAMIN STILLERMAN

ABOUT THE AUTHOR

Melissa Lozada-Oliva is the child of Guatemalan and Colombian immigrants. She co-hosts the podcast *Say More* and is a member of the band Meli and the Specs. She holds an MFA in poetry from NYU and her writing has been featured in *Remezcla, PAPER, The Guardian, The BreakBeat Poets Vol. 4, Wirecutter, Vulture, Bustle, Glamour, The Huffington Post, Muzzle Magazine, The Poetry Project, Audible,* and *BBC Mundo.* She is from Massachusetts and lives in New York City.